BODY ON THE TRAIN

A RITA PATEL MYSTERY

By Catherine Cooper

Chapter

1

Friday 22ⁿᵈ April 2016 6pm
2 hours missing

The problem with Trouble, Rita Patel thought, was that it never bothered to announce itself. If it sent you a 'save the date' card, or messaged you, then you would have a chance to be prepared. If she had known it was coming, she could have worn more suitable clothes. She could have got an extension on her second year uni work. She could have changed her status and alerted her contacts. She could have left a message for the people she loved the most - her mother, her brothers, her boyfriend, Jacob, and Priya, her best friend since school days. She could have sold the tickets to the gig she had been looking forward to. But Trouble wasn't thoughtful. It arrived without warning. It didn't give you a chance to pack and say your farewells.

Saturday 23ʳᵈ April 2016 3pm
I day missing

"This is stressing me out! Rita's really missing?" Priya Shah was sitting on the bed in her shared student house in Oxford, leaning against a pile of brightly coloured cushions. She was talking agitatedly on her phone screen to Mohal, Rita's older brother, both their faces leaning in close in their anxiety. Priya was speaking so loudly that her housemate, Ayeesha, came from the next room to stand in the doorway and raise her eyebrows questioningly. She saw with concern that Priya's long brown black hair was hanging loosely over her oval face, and noticed that she was passing her fingers through her locks nervously as she spoke. Mohal could see the anxiety on Priya's face as he looked at her head framed by cushions in richly coloured Indian fabrics which Priya had acquired in the covered market in the city. By contrast, from what Priya could see, Mohal seemed to be perched on an unmade bed. There were posters on the wall behind him showing motor bikes mounted by men in fringed leather jackets and aviator Ray-Bans. The decor suggested to her that he was in the room in the Patel family home in Oadby, Leicester, which belonged to his younger brother, Nayan.

Priya looked up at Ayeesha and grimaced. She couldn't believe that, until Mohal's call, apart from her studies, all she had been focussed on was celebrating the day as the 46th anniversary of Earth Day. She had helped Ayeesha to distribute flyers and post messages on line – 'Stand up! Join Up! Take Action!'. As part of the worldwide events to demonstrate support for environmental protection, they were organising a tree planting in the communal gardens near their house in Henley Street. Now her concerns about the planet were eclipsed by the dark shadow of worry for her friend. Seeing her anxiety, Ayeesha walked across to the bed and sat beside Priya, sharing a view of Mohal's face on the phone screen and offering him a vague wave of her hand, which he did not seem to notice.

"Yeh. No word from her since she left the house yesterday." Mohal's voice was tight, as if stuck in the back of his throat. As the older brother, he had felt heavy with responsibility for the family ever since their father had died, a sadness which had occurred barely a year ago. How would his father have coped with this news he wondered?

"Jacob doesn't know where she is?" Priya mentioned

Rita's boyfriend of a few months, an actor who did casual jobs around their home town of Leicester when 'resting'.

"No" Mohal confirmed, shaking his head firmly, making his thick dark hair quiver. "She was going to meet him as a surprise, she was all dressed up", Nayan said. "But she never got to the Coop store where he was working."

"Nayan was the last to see her? But he's like so…." Priya stopped, not wanting to articulate her concerns. Nayan was just finishing school; he was two years younger than her friend but, in Priya's opinion, as she and Rita had often privately agreed, way younger in maturity. Rita had good observational skills and an interest in other people, which was why she liked to get involved in solving mysteries. Lacking those attributes, it was unlikely, she thought, that Nayan he would have noticed anything that might be a clue to his sister's whereabouts.

"Yeh, I know." Mohal got the picture. "He was the only one in the house when she went out." he admitted.

"Your mum must be going crazy!" Priya's eyes were wide with alarm as she tried to imagine the atmosphere at Rita's home where she had been catching up with her family before returning to Warwick University for the summer term of history studies and exams.

"Tell me about it!" Mohal shook his head again as he recalled Padma, their mother, practically wearing a path into the carpet of the living room in their house at 10 Elm Drive that morning as she scrolled through her phone, trying every number she could think of, after Rita had failed to come home the previous night. As he pictured the scene, Ayeesha and Priya could see Mohal's jaw twitching with suppressed emotion.

"What about the police? Do they have anything to say?" Ayeesha chipped in.

Mohal's eyes opened wider with a startled looked, as if he was noticing Ayeesha's presence for the first time, then he shrugged. "They weren't interested at first, but when they learnt who she was they said they would send someone." Just as he spoke, Priya could hear a door bell ringing in the house behind him. She saw Mohal look round at the sound.

"Got to go" he said.

"Sure" Priya swallowed hard and coughed, trying to ensure that her voice did not betray her. "If she doesn't get in touch soon, I'll come back to Leicester." she added in a hoarse but determined whisper. "I can revise for my exams there as easily as in Oxford and I may be able to help."

After the call ended, Priya turned to Ayeesha and let out a cry of anguish. "Where can Rita be?" she wailed.

Chapter

2

"A railroad is like a lie. You have to keep building it to make it stand."

Mark Twain

Saturday 23rd April 2016 3.30pm
1 day missing

At 10 Elm Drive, Mohal pocketed his phone and left his brother's room, clattering down the spiral staircase and striding to the white and grey kitchen where an anxious group had gathered. Usually Saturdays for Mohal, his brother and sister, when home, were relaxed affairs. Sometimes their mother would be at the dental surgery which she ran, in which case her offspring could stroll down to breakfast, on a schedule and in an attire relaxed to suit themselves. When, instead, Padma was at home, her morning would be taken up with cooking while glued to Saturday Kitchen and Master Chef on the TV, before it was taken over by football, in which case she enticed her children down with cooking smells too good to ignore. But there had been no surgery and no cookery programmes that day, and her sons were discreetly monitoring the football via their phones rather than on the television screen.

"#findrita is trending!" Nayan was announcing to his aunt, Jaina, as Mohal came into the room. Jaina was loading the dishwasher with cups from the tea she had insisted on making. Jaina preferred to keep herself busy to hide her concern. She did not know how she would cope if one of her twins, Shona and Shreya, a few years younger than Nayan, were to go missing.

"But it's only been 24 hours" her husband, Bandhu, had said to reassure her, "Young people go off for days without remembering to tell anyone. It's the norm today. They only think of themselves."

"Not Rita" Jaina had replied. "She always keeps in touch with Padma, more so since her father died, she knows her mother worries. Besides, there are so many ways to keep in contact these days. Youngsters are never off their phones. It's just not like Rita." she had insisted.

"People are posting sightings!" As if to prove Jaina right, her nephew, Nayan, was on his phone now, scrolling through the screen as he leant against one of the worktops. He was so engrossed he did not notice his mother enter the kitchen in the company of two strangers, a man and a woman, both sporting dark quilted jackets and combat trousers. Padma gestured for them to sit at the table while Nayan looked up briefly, then went on with his internet search, scarcely acknowledging the visitors.

"There's one in Dover, getting a ferry to France; there's one in York, at the railway museum, in the company of two men; another person thinks they saw her in Norwich with a hen party!" Rita's younger brother went on in a voice rising with excitement.

"Please, Nayan" Padma pleaded, removing her glasses from her snub-shaped nose and setting them on the table so she could wipe the damp from her eyes. The reality of the situation had hit her when she opened the door. Seeing the police officers had caused a wave of feelings to rise up from her stomach to her chest and throat and then to her eyes.

"Sit down with us. That's enough!" she rebuked her youngest in a staccato whisper, paused to take in a breath, then continued in an assertive tone, the tone she sometimes used to bring order at the dental practice, which, since her husband's untimely death, she now ran on her own.

"We are worried enough! We don't want to hear that

people may have seen her from Cornwall to Edinburgh. I want Rita, I want my daughter, to get in touch. To tell me she's all right." Padma spoke firmly.

Silenced by the note in her voice, which he recognised as meaning the situation was serious, Nayan slumped down next to his brother, whose height he was rapidly approaching himself, having had a recent growth spurt, and waited for his mother to introduce the newcomers.

"This is.." Padma began, "I'm sorry I have forgotten your names, I am not myself today, forgive me!" she shook her head in her confusion. This was not like her she thought.

"That's all right" said the woman, unzipping her jacket and turning to place it on the back of her chair before taking out a Blackberry from her bag.

"Hello" she said, using her hands to tighten the pony tail in which her light brown hair was tamed, and then, before she sat down, gesturing to the room as if at a briefing, "I am Detective Inspector Sue Foster and this is Detective Sergeant David Hann." She indicated the rather heavily built officer who had placed himself on a chair to her left. Jaina nodded at the introductions, concerned for a moment as to whether the chair would take the officer's weight. She found herself recalling somewhat unkindly a recent news item about the average size of police uniforms going up; perhaps they spent more time on computers rather than the beat these days, she thought. The Detective Sergeant, who went in for a more traditional means of keeping records than his boss, placed a notebook on the table before pressing the end of his pen with his thumb in preparation.

"Where are my manners?" Padma was still agitated, "Would you like some refreshment? Tea perhaps?" she offered.

"Water would be fine thanks, Mrs Patel" Sue Foster replied before DS Hann could express a preference for anything else.

"I'll get it" Jaina stood up and showed her familiarity with her sister's kitchen by opening a cupboard door to take out several tumblers which she filled with chilled water from the American style fridge-freezer.

"Rita can't stay hidden for long, Mum." Nayan broke in, unable to restrain himself for long and he looked hopefully at the officers. "No one can these days. There's CCTV everywhere. The police can monitor any use of her bank account and credit cards, and there's her phone. That will leave a signal. Pity she didn't have tracking on it. But it was a full moon last night so the light was good. If she was around somewhere, someone is bound to have seen her, there were lots of people on the streets because of the beacons for the Queen's birthday." Nayan's optimistic ideas finally came to an end.

"Yes, but she could easily have been taken away in the middle of a crowd, with no evidence." Padma countered, "And with all this – what do you call it, 'social media' - she must know we need to hear from her. The fact that she hasn't got in touch suggests she may have come to some harm! I know she would reply to my calls if she could. It is her birthday soon and I can't bear to think…." Padma sucked in a breath noisily, wanting not to cry, "If only your father were still alive! He might know where to look for her!" Despite her best intentions, Padma had to start dabbing at her eyes again. Jaina leant over to set a tumbler of water in front of her sister, pausing to stroke her hand sympathetically.

"Priya said she would come to help." Mohal spoke, trying to supply some reassurance. "That's a friend of Rita's." he explained to the officers. "She and I can go to some of Rita's haunts, see if anyone can remember anything. Sammi, another friend of hers, will be doing the same at Warwick Uni, and in Leamington, where she lives in term time." he added.

Padma sighed and nodded, brushing from her face hair which was curly like her daughter's, and which she dyed these days to keep its nutty brown colour. Mohal's mention of Warwick reminded her that Rita should be getting ready to return for the start of the new term on Monday. Where could she be?

What if Rita had got involved in one of her investigations? she was thinking. Her impetuous daughter liked to try to solve mysteries and had helped the police in the past with several murders. Her curiosity had got her into trouble before. Padma's deepest fear was that Rita had come across the wrong person. Could she be lying somewhere in pain or unconscious? Why wouldn't she contact them?

Chapter

3

"When a train goes through a tunnel and it gets dark, you don't throw away the ticket and jump off. You sit still and trust the engineer."

Corrie Ten Boom

Saturday 23rd April 2016 4pm
1 day missing

DI Foster nodded to her colleague. She had been sceptical about starting inquiries into this girl's disappearance so soon and thought it was probably a waste of resources. So much police time was taken up with missing persons these days that normally the Leicestershire force would advise allowing a few days before they took action. In the previous year forces across the UK had dealt with over 300,000 missing person cases. That equated to 838 a day or one person being reported missing every 2 minutes. How could the local forces, or the Missing Persons Bureau at the National Crime Agency, check every case, with that volume? The recession since the banking crisis seemed to have made things worse. Financial problems were a major factor in people losing their jobs, their homes, their families, and their ties to their communities, the Inspector knew.

In Sue Foster's experience, which she had not been shy to share with DS Hann in the car on the way to Elm Drive, most adults usually turned up unharmed and wondering what the fuss was about, especially young women with over-fussy mothers. But there had been a call to the police station from another DI, Jamie Bridge, who was on a training course in the Lake District. He had seen the comments about Rita

Patel on Twitter. He had reminded them that Rita had helped the force with inquiries in the past; he sounded concerned. So here they were.

"Who lives in the house?" was her first question.

Padma pointed to herself and to Rita's brothers.

"No one else?" the DI pressed.

"Not since their father, my husband, died last year." Padma said in a small voice. "We did have a lodger for a while, a Dr Sharma. He came to help out at the dental surgery. He moved out when his wife..oh dear!" Padma stopped abruptly and reached for the box of tissues on the table.

"Dr Sharma and his family live in Syston now." Jaina broke in to help out her sister while she regained her composure, mentioning a town a few miles from the centre of Leicester and popular with people who work in the city.

"Except that his wife was sadly killed only last week." Mohal added in a soft voice by way of explanation. DI Foster looked surprised, then understanding spread across her face as Mohal continued, "She disturbed some burglars at her house."

The officers exchanged a look of recognition. The shocking recent death of this young mother at the hands of thieves, who, when she had disturbed them, had fatally smashed a mirror over her head in their haste to escape, was being investigated by another team. They had not realised there would be any connection with this missing person case. DS Hann's pen was making notes swiftly now.

"I know a bit about it. I have been covering the story for the paper. I work for the Mercury." Mohal went on, mentioning the local daily paper and wanting to demonstrate that his knowledge had been gleaned professionally and not out of prurience.

"I don't think he could have anything to do with this." Padma was saying, referring to Dr Sharma.

DS Hann looked up when he had finished writing. He

asked Nayan to describe his sister's clothes when she had left the house at 3.30 the previous afternoon, over 24 hours ago.

"She was showing off in her new Leicester blue sari." Nayan volunteered.

Padma frowned at her son. Criticism of his sister was not allowed at this time.

"She was excited. She was going to dress up to meet her boyfriend." Rita's mother explained.

"She took her black jacket and her satchel bag." Nayan added.

"And on her feet?" DS Hann asked.

"Oh, I don't know!" Nayan thought he had done well to remember the bag and jacket. When Rita had left the house, he had been preoccupied with the Leicester City website, looking to see what their manager, Ranieri, had to say about the weekend's fixture against Swansea. Not content with getting clear of relegation from the Premier League, the team had surpassed itself and secured a place in the Champions League next season, an achievement that seemed to bring a tear to the manager's eye and to justify his often-used comment, "Justa keep on dreaming". For the first time, it had seemed that Ranieri was beginning to acknowledge the unlikely possibility that the Premier League title could be within their grasp. Leicester City were becoming everyone's second team as they watched to see if the miracle would happen. The City itself was starting to hold its collective breath and souvenirs were on sale everywhere, including saris in the team colours. The task of winning the Premiership would be made more difficult by the sending off of their main striker, Vardy, in last week's match against West Ham. So, while Nayan had acknowledged his sister's departure, with all these concerns he hadn't given her his full attention, just as her friend Priya had feared.

"I expect she wore her gold sandals." Padma said. "I can't see them in her room." she explained.

Questioned by DI Foster, the table occupants confirmed what Padma had said about Rita's mood and intentions the previous day.

"She was going to surprise her boyfriend, Jacob. It was his birthday. She was taking him for a meal on Belgrave Road."

"She seemed the usual Rita, full of life and looking forward to meeting up with Jacob. They don't see each other much with her being at uni."

"But they skype every day and keep in touch"

"OK." the DI nodded and the two officers stood at the same time. "I think we have enough for now. We'll make some initial inquiries. It is very early to be concerned, but we will do some preliminary work just in case." DI Foster summarised.

"If you could just show me her room and allow DS Hann to look round the garage and the garden?"

Padma and her sister exchanged a mystified look. Why the garage and the garden? they wondered.

"I'll show you her room." Mohal offered to the Detective Inspector, while Nayan ushered the Detective Sergeant outside through the door from the kitchen to the garden, accompanied by Padma's commentary explaining that until recently the garden had been carefully cultivated by her husband and was now maintained to a lesser standard by his sons, with occasional help from others, including Dr Sharma. She stopped then, recalling the sad death of her former lodger's wife. She was starting to think this might not be a coincidence. A cloud of bad luck seemed to be engulfing them all.

Chapter

4

Saturday 23rd April 2016 5pm
1 day missing

Standing in Rita's bedroom, her hands on her hips, Sue Foster surveyed the contents with her eyes before touching anything. The room was painted in shades of turquoise and grey, on top of a chest of drawers there was an array of jewellery and cosmetics, by the bed there were books and boxes stacked on the floor, and, behind the wardrobe door, she found hanging neatly a series of shirts, skirts and jeans. There was nothing to suggest that the occupant had left in a hurry, or that she had planned to leave for any time at all. It was as if Rita had just stepped out for a few hours, nothing more.

A lap top lay on the bed, she noted. "Don't suppose you know the password for that?" she pointed to the machine.

"Bosworth2208" came the answer from Mohal surprisingly quickly. "Really?" the Detective Inspector wrote down the code and bagged the computer, tucking it under her arm.

"Yeh. If you knew Rita, you'd crack it at once. It's the date of the battle in 1485 when Richard III was killed." Mohal explained. "Rita is always banging on about it. I don't even like history but thanks to her I know that date, and that 22 August was also the date in 1642 when King Charles I raised his standard at Nottingham, kicking off the English civil war.

A very significant date, Rita would say." He smiled as these memories conjured up a picture of his sister.

"Very interesting." Sue Foster said in a flat voice which suggested she was not particularly engaged with this subject.

"Where were you yesterday afternoon and evening?" her tone became sharp.

"Oh, I was out, reporting for the paper on the beacon lighting for the Queen's 90th birthday. I went to various villages. I had a photographer with me the whole time." Mohal felt he should give a full answer. There was no point in the police following up false leads.

The DI nodded and swiftly typed something on her Blackberry before she changed to a friendlier approach, seeking Mohal's help.

"What kind of phone does she have?" she asked him and he explained that Rita had an iPhone and an iPad which she always kept with her.

"DI Foster!" DS Hann called up the spiral staircase to his boss.

"I think you should look at this!" he added urgently. The Inspector and Mohal swiftly left Rita's room and made their way down the stairway and out of the house to see what had caught the attention of the Sergeant.

* * *

"If you would stay by the entrance." DI Foster requested of the family, who gathered together by the garden door, looking like a wedding group waiting for a photograph. They watched curiously while she accompanied David Hann to a patch of the garden to the right of the lawn.

"It's been dug recently" the Sergeant told his colleague, covering his mouth as he spoke, like a doubles player in tennis, so that no one could lip read. Together they studied an area of soil roughly 2 metres by 1 metre. DI Foster stared at the spot thoughtfully and nodded her head. It looked like she was going to have to take the investigation up a notch. She sighed as she thought how unpopular that would make her with the Superintendent, who had been hoping this matter would be resolved quickly and favourably. The force's resources were stretched already and now it looked like they might need a full team, on overtime. It would make a big dent in the month's budget.

"When was that area dug out?" DI Foster asked as the officers returned to the family.

Padma took on the task of explaining that Dr Sharma had taken responsibility for the vegetable patch. He was planning to grow onions and to put up bamboo wigwams to grow beans. She told the Inspector that Dr Sharma had been keen to help with the garden. Everything had been overtaken by the tragic events concerning his wife, of course. But, DI Foster was surprised to learn, the dentist and former lodger had returned only the previous evening to finish the preparatory digging, saying his children were with friends and that it would help him to take advantage of the dry weather and do something useful.

As Sue Foster indicated to DS Hann to make another of his notes, she became distracted by the shrill sound of her phone and turned away from the group to take the call.

When the conversation ended, she called DS Hann over. "I don't like the look of this." she said with her back to the family group, shaking her head; it was starting to look like she and the DS were going to have a long shift. "There are no indications that Rita Patel has been admitted to hospital or any police station. What's more a Big Issue seller reports seeing an Asian woman being forced into a car in the town centre, on Halford Street, yesterday afternoon. It needs checking out. Say nothing to the family yet." the DI warned, then went on, her voice full of concern, "Her phone isn't sending out a signal. The Halford Street area in town was the last time it pinged a mast. Meanwhile we have this patch in the garden. I think we need a team here for a full search. Reassure the family it's just routine."

"Yes boss." Hann said, wondering how he was going to achieve that.

While DI Foster made her excuses, and left to make several calls, DS Hann tried as best he could to explain tactfully that the house was about to be invaded by a SOCO team, just as soon as they could be scrambled, and that nothing should be touched in the meantime. Mohal was just in time to catch his mother as her legs started to give way from under her.

* * *

A few hours later, an unusual sight greeted Mrs Banerjee and Mr Mehta, who were both peering cautiously out of the windows of their homes on the quiet suburban road that was Elm Drive. Lined on both sides with detached and semi- detached houses, which had been built in the rush to meet post war demand for housing in the 1950s, the hastily completed structures had undergone various processes of improvement since and now boasted mainly paved fronts where gardens had been, and extensions in every direction you could think of, encasing garages, utility and games rooms and many other luxuries undreamt of at the time of construction. Mrs Banerjee and Mr Mehta could observe that several vehicles were now parked in the vicinity of number 10, from which had spilled a number of people in a variety of outfits, like an ill-assorted fancy dress party. Some wore uniforms, others were dressed head to foot in white or blue, looking like giant Teletubbies. These figures pulled coloured covers on over their shoes before they entered the house or the garden. A uniformed officer stood guard at the front door.

19

* * *

Unlike her neighbours, Padma preferred not to watch what was going on in the street and waited in Rita's room, which overlooked the garden at the back of the house, while officers carried out a thorough search of it. Standing at the window, her right hand coiled in tension round the back of her neck, she had a good view of the antics in the garden where a blue tent had been erected over the vegetable patch and a generator was throbbing to supply light to the digging process. She shivered at the thought that her daughter's body could be lying there, so close to home. It was unthinkable.

Chapter

5

"Neither a wise man nor a brave man lies down on the tracks of history to wait for the train of the future to run over him."

Dwight D. Eisenhower

Tuesday 26th April 2016 1pm
4 days missing

When the search teams had gone, leaving no trace of their presence other than some dustings of powder, a bath panel that wasn't quite straight any more, and an extra well- dug vegetable patch,10 Elm Drive was a strangely quiet place. It missed Rita's voice, her energy, and the excitement of her presence. When she was in the house, she presented a restless sense of curiosity and she goaded and encouraged her brothers and mother, and anyone else present, into helping with her latest investigation, whether into a historical subject or an unsolved mystery. When not at home, she bombarded it with messages and calls, chatting screen to screen with Padma in the evenings in between doing her uni work or calling one of her brothers in the early hours.

Now the phones and tablets were quiet. The tidiness of the kitchen spoke of the absence. There were no mugs of cold mint tea left by the sink as Rita departed suddenly on another mission; there were no half- eaten packets of her favourite wafer biscuits left forgotten on the white table. Padma noticed that Rita's absence affected her brothers in different ways. The younger one spent a lot of his time in his room doodling #Fearless over and over again in honour of his Leicester City heroes and to give himself courage while they waited for news of Rita. Padma's eldest child was mostly on the road in the county with his job, all the while listening out for information from other reporters that might give a clue as to what had happened to his sister. The crime reporters were particularly depressing, Mohal had reported. Apparently, a high percentage of missing people were never found, "If they want to stay hidden, they stay hidden." he was told. Did Rita want to stay hidden? Mohal did not think so, but he kept this part of the information to himself. The family met at the table for meals which Padma half-heartedly prepared, their minds constantly distracted by worry. Generally, they sat in silence as they ate, all possible words having been spoken.

Nayan had broken the quiet at the meal on Sunday to remind them about the football team's win the previous day. He had jumped around the kitchen, his arms waving, as he sang the crowd's chant of "Four nil to the one-man team" which was their riposte to critics who had claimed that City could not win without their striker, Vardy, who was sitting in the stands, working out a two-match ban. Two large banners had been unfurled at the Kingpower ground bearing the words "History Makes Us Who We are". Jamie Vardy and the striker Riyad Mahrez had been whisked away afterwards by helicopter for the Professional Footballers Association dinner. Although the stadium was no stranger to the helicopter these days, it being the means by which the Thai owners of the club chose to arrive and leave, often accompanied by Buddhist monks in their saffron robes, the drama of the players' departure added to the feeling of excitement and speculation at the football ground and around the City. A 'Back the Blues' day was planned for the following Friday, when many buildings and landmarks would be turned blue. A lot of neutrals were starting to think the unthinkable and get behind Leicester who had been 5000 – 1 to win the League at the start of the season. "We're going to win the League. And you don't believe us!" Nayan had chanted as he moved to the living room.

But that was Sunday. When there was still no news by Tuesday, the family's mood was subdued. Rita was uppermost in their minds and the last person to be mentioned. Their sighs and anxious glances at phone screens while they tried to eat showed where their thoughts were centred. Although it had yielded no clues, the intense police activity at the weekend had spooked them all. It seemed to give credence to their concerns. It was official confirmation that there was something serious to be worried about. Nayan tried to apply the exhortations of Ranieri, the Leicester manager, to his team as they faced the prospect of a fixture against Manchester United the next week, still without Vardy. They must remain consistent, he had said, and they must fight. Nayan tried to keep this attitude in his mind; they must be consistent, they must fight for his sister. Like the Foxes they must be Fearless.

Detective Constable Gardner had been appointed as the police family liaison officer. She knew Rita from a previous investigation; in fact, Rita had saved her life. She checked in with the Patels twice a day as a matter of routine, and more often if there was anything to report. But there was nothing to report. The sighting by the Big Issue seller, which DI Foster had mentioned to her Sergeant on Saturday, had been investigated and the family had been made aware of it. It was a lead the police were trying to follow. Unfortunately, the seller's eyesight and memory were not of the best, so that they could describe neither the car into which the woman in a sari had apparently been forced, nor the other people involved. There were no other leads. The Patels' sister and daughter seemed to have been removed from sight in the centre of Leicester, leaving no clues as to why, or where she had been taken.

"What would Rita do?" Priya had commented to Mohal on WhatsApp just before the latest family meal started. That was a good question he mused as he chewed a corner of his samosa. He would call Priya. Maybe two heads would be better than one.

Wednesday 27th April 2016 11am
5 days missing

Although it was the spring term at Oxford, where she was studying, or Trinity term as they called it there, Priya Shah, restless until her friend could be found, had come back to Leicester. She was walking slowly past the independent boutiques and niche shops in The Lanes area of the town centre. She turned into the newly refurbished and award-winning Silver Arcade in order to continue her phone conversation while browsing in the shop windows. She spied a quaint tea room and, despite herself, thought she must tell Rita about it. That was what absence did to you, she realised. It was like that phantom limb syndrome of amputees, which they had studied on her medical course. Just because you knew rationally that something or someone was not there, it didn't stop you from getting feelings or thinking about them.

Priya wore a green top over brown jeans and boots, with a loose-fitting black jumper wrapped around her neck and draped over her back. She had her earphones in order to hear what Mohal was saying to her on the phone. Although she was due to meet him later, she was keen to get up to date on the search for Rita.

"Still no sign of her? No word at all?" Priya was aghast. She knew about the abduction theory – DC Gardner had explained the sighting to the family and Mohal had broken the possibility to her. She hoped it was wrong, just a bad dream. She so wanted good news and to be reunited with her friend. Now dread was sitting like a stone in the pit of her stomach.

"Lots of responses on Twitter and Facebook. The police are chasing them up. But they are not hopeful. It's been more than half a week! If she could, she would have got in touch by now, I'm sure." Exasperation sighed down the phone from Mohal's end to Priya's.

Priya's sigh echoed in return. She felt bad that, before catching up with Mohal she was going to a nail bar. She would be attending to her appearance while her friend could be in serious trouble, could be lying somewhere, injured or worse.

"It must be something to do with Rita finding that body, and the murder trial." Mohal was saying, "It's too much of a coincidence that she has disappeared and so has the accused - the victim's daughter - as well as her brother." he told Priya.

"You mean Tanisha Kahn and - what was her brother called?" Priya asked.

"Lateef," Mohal answered, "Rita gave her evidence last November in Tanisha's trial for the murder of her father, Afzal Kahn. The jury returned a not guilty verdict, if you remember."

Priya nodded her head, "I do, vaguely." she said, "But that was months ago. Why would they disappear now, and what could it have to do with Rita?" she puzzled.

"I heard from a reporter on the paper." Mohal said," The police are trying to keep the Kahns' disappearances hush hush, but the news is starting to get out. It will reopen speculation as to who did kill Afzal Kahn, if it wasn't his daughter. He was poisoned, if you remember."

"Yes." Priya was recalling some of details which Rita had told her. "Aconite,wasn't it?" Priya remembered that aspect. Poisons were a particular interest of hers in her medical studies.

"I think so, yeh." Mohal was less sure of the detail. It was a few months since he had sat in the court listening to the case for his newpaper report. "There has been speculation as to why no one else was charged after her acquittal." he told Rita's friend, "Her leaving the country..." he went on.

Priya interrupted, "Wait a minute. Are you saying they have left the UK? Tanisha has gone abroad, and her brother too?" her voice rose with surprise. Mohal had all her attention now and her interest in the goods on display in the shops had disappeared.

"Apparently, yeh. That's what the reporter told me." Mohal confirmed.

"You don't ..like..think Rita's with them?" Priya was aghast.

Chapter

6

"Over my desk hangs a poster from The Railway Children that my husband had framed for me. It is so lovely to see the children smiling as they run down the railway track. "

Dinah Sheridan

Wednesday 27ᵗʰ April 2017 11.15am
5 days missing

"Nah!" Mohal protested quickly. "It's not like she knew them." He replied with more assurance than he was feeling. It had not occurred to him before Priya spoke that Rita might also have gone abroad, willingly or otherwise. This was starting to look sinister.

"Well what then? Why would them leaving the UK and Rita disappearing – perhaps being taken if that's what's happened- be connected? She only gave evidence reluctantly didn't she? Why would anyone want to remove her now? What good would it do?" Priya finally stopped for breath.

"I don't know." Mohal conceded. "It is a coincidence, though." he paused before answering her other question, "You're right that Rita didn't want to give evidence. She didn't believe in the prosecution case, but she was told she had no choice."

"They thought her evidence added to the case against Tanisha Kahn, the victim's daughter?" Priya asked, swapping her phone from one hand to the other.

"Rita said she thought she had glimpsed someone in the carriage where the dead man had been, and the police used what she said because it fitted their case, or at least that's what Rita said to me." Mohal told her.

Priya was racking her brains now, trying to recall some of what Rita had said to her about the incident and about giving evidence. She wished she had paid more attention at the time. Rita was always telling her things. How was she to know this might be important?

"She seemed nervous in the witness box." Mohal told Priya, "I go to court a lot for the paper and see people giving evidence. Some are cocky and over-confident, some are so scared they can barely speak. Rita was shaking – I could see her hands trembling as she clung to the edge of the box. And the defence barrister was quite hostile."

"Poor Rita." Priya had not been able to attend the trial. The autumn had been a busy time for her pre-clinical course at Merton College, part of Oxford University. She had not even found much to chat with her friend much over that period, and had missed their conversations, especially Rita's quirky interest, to Priya's mind, in history. She had once discussed with Priya, for example, how William Harvey, who discovered the circulation of the blood, had studied at Merton, and the fact that the medical society was named after him. Who else among her friends would be interested in that?

Now she thought about it, even when she had spared a few days after the trial to get together with Rita, her friend had been strangely quiet about the court case. The two had taken a short break in France. As Priya remembered it, Rita had been reticent about what happened when she gave evidence and, anyway, other events had eclipsed whatever might have been her personal ordeal at the murder trial.

Now, as she gazed through large glass windows at ideas for gifts, which were making no impression on her, Priya asked Mohal to describe what her friend had been through. Perhaps it would provide the key to what had happened to Rita.

"She, the barrister, tried to say that Rita's memory was at fault." he explained.

"That's bad!" Priya was indignant. "Rita was a witness. She wasn't on trial!"

"I know. But that's how things work in court. It's not the pursuit of truth, but who can convince the jury." Mohal explained.

"So, she told them about the train, about the man, the body, Afzal Kahn as it turned out, falling onto her as she opened the carriage door?" Priya recited the basic facts as she knew them.

"Yes. Two witnesses from the Great Central Railway had already given evidence. They explained the timetable for the train that day in July last year. How people on the station in Loughborough were watching the steam train arrive from Leicester. The guard said there were 10 people on board, including Rita, Nayan and my Mum. They had planned to have a picnic before getting the train back. When the train pulled in,they split up. Nayan and my Mum wanted to see the engine up close,while Rita went towards the back of the train so she could check the timetable,which was on the station wall, for the return trip. That was when she saw what she thought was a man struggling with a carriage door and, well, you know Rita, she went to help. Just like my sister! She acts first and thinks second."

Mohal paused while the two of them on either end of the phone call pictured Rita and thought how eager she was and how much they missed her.

"So, Rita opened the train door and Afzal Kahn fell out, knocking her to the ground?" Priya broke the silence.

"Yeh. The pathologist had said he was already dead by then, or as good as." Mohal confirmed. "Poisoned.Tests found aconite in his flask of soup"

"Grisly" Priya said, stroking her black brown hair, which was tied in the nape of her neck and draped over her left shoulder, as she replied. She had read articles about aconite. Also known as monkshood, or wolfsbane, it was a poison known since ancient times and a favourite method of execution used by the Romans.Within minutes to a few hours, its ingestion affected the nervous system causing life threatening changes to the victim's heart rhythm. The patient might also complain of dizziness, numbness and tingling, or abdominal pain, and suffer from vomiting.Such poisonings were common in Asia since aconite was used in Chinese medicine for joint and muscle pain. From what she had heard, the poison had had a rapid and fatal effect on Afzhal Kahn.

"Yes. Quite a shock for Rita. As the defence barrister pointed out." Mohal agreed.

"Why did Rita open the door? Wasn't there a guard or someone to do that?" Priya checked.

"Well, yeh, that's what the company said in their evidence. A railway official called Daniel Smith ran up to where Rita was on the ground…"

"Under the body." Priya interjected.

"Under the body" Mohal agreed. "He seemed more bothered that she had opened the door to begin with, according to Nayan. He and Mum were hurrying towards Rita, too, at that point, rushing behind this Mr. Smith who was running and blowing his whistle at the same time, not an easy thing to do." Mohal told Priya.

"So, they were all racing towards Rita, who was prone on the platform in front of the open train door with this dead man pinning her to the ground?" Priya narrowed her eyes, trying to picture the scene.

"Yeh. And she thought she saw another person getting out of the carriage on the other side." Mohal confirmed, "Trouble is, no one else saw them. That's why her evidence was vital to the CPS." Mohal explained.

"And the person, the figure, was dressed in black?" Priya

tried to remember the little that Rita had said.

"That was her impression. Look, the police wanted to charge Tanisha Kahn, who prepared her father's food every day. He was on a special diet I think I heard. But there were no fingerprints at all on the flask, which had contained the poisoned soup. The CPS seemed to think it added weight to their case, if they could show that Tanisha was on the train when he drank from the flask. That is why the defence barrister gave Rita such a hard time."

"And was it Tanisha that she saw? What did Rita say in her evidence?" Priya, leaning against a wall now, was finding it comforting, in a strange way, to talk over the case with Mohal. It offered a distraction from fretting about Rita and made her feel closer to her friend.

"Rita was the only one to see another figure. She thought she saw the person escape using the carriage door on the other side. According to Rita, once she had been pinned to the ground and had the wind taken out of her sails it took a couple of minutes - or so it seemed - for everyone around to realise what was going on. Then the guard was running and whistling, followed by Mum and my brother. There was a group of children who started shrieking and were ushered away by their teachers. An elderly man kept shouting to be told what was going on."

"What did Nayan say happened?" Priya did not put much faith in Rita's younger brother noticing anything, but you never knew.

"Nayan says he thought at first that the man was attacking Rita, and he dropped the picnic in his rush to help her. It was only when he got close, and the guard had touched the man, that Nayan realised the man couldn't move. Nayan helped the guard to lift him up a bit and Rita wriggled from under him. Rita told the guard to call the police. Mum was there by then, wringing her hands and wailing "Oh Rita! How do these things happen to you! What am I going to do about you! etc. So, the person, whoever was in the carriage, could have escaped in all the confusion without being seen, I suppose." Mohal conceded.

"But Rita didn't say it was a woman in a burka she saw? Which was what the police case suggested, to make it fit with Tanisha?" Priya wanted to be sure.

"What she said exactly was 'black and flowing, like a coat.'" Mohal confirmed. "But this was the middle of July. It was too warm and dry for a proper coat. Which supported the burka theory, I guess."

"The jury didn't convict?" Priya checked again. She thought she remembered Rita getting a phone call to that effect when they were together in Paris after the trial. It was hard to remember because of what happened after that.

"No. The judge said they had to be sure beyond reasonable doubt that Tanisha had obtained and administered the poison. The CPS had no evidence of that. It was all circumstantial. The Kahns are a family of pharmacists. They run a chemist shop on the Narborough Road. Tanisha had worked there at weekends and understood about drugs and stuff. But there was no evidence she got any medicines from her place of work. The CPS tried to suggest she had got it on the internet, but they had no evidence of that either."

"And Tanisha said she was at home at the time? When the train was traveling from Leicester to Loughborough?" Priya asked.

"Yes. Tanisha could not support her alibi though. She was at home alone at the time. But, anyway, the jury weren't convinced by the case. They acquitted her."

"The police can't have been happy about that!" Priya exclaimed.

"No doubt they weren't. Rita's evidence was not enough!" Mohal agreed.

"Oh dear, all that ordeal for Rita for nothing." said Priya. Then she took a breath, this conversation about her brave friend had deepened her resolve to act, "We have to find out what has happened to her." she said to Mohal, determinedly. "We must think like her. WWRD! What would Rita do ?"

Chapter

7

"It doesn't seem like you're living a life, it's almost like you're travelling on a train with the destination unknown."

Sanhita Baruah

Wednesday 27th April 2016 2pm
5 days missing

An hour later, her nails an immaculate shade of Leicester City blue, the only colour to wear in the City at that moment, Priya was standing by a statue of William Wyggeston, a local benefactor and one of four figures immortalised at the corners which form the base of the Clock Tower in the heart of Leicester city centre. Shoppers milled about her, moving from the High Cross shopping centre to the Haymarket and back, and workers marched purposefully, often with lap top bags clinging to their backs or papers tucked under their arms, like an office army on the move. A few groups of teenagers were starting to gather in corners and doorways. Some canvassers were encouraging passers-by to take leaflets about the forthcoming EU referendum. Red T-shirts were worn by the Leave adherents, blue by the Remainers. Their rivalry was good-natured as they exchanged jokes with one another and members of the public. Priya had seen on a rolling news programme as she passed a TV shop that David Cameron had been talking about the referendum in Prime Minister's Questions. As she scanned the horizon for Mohal, allegedly on his way so they could retrace Rita's last known footsteps, hoping to jog someone's memory or get some new clues, Priya hoped relations between the sides in the referendum debate would be as amicable after the vote.

Smiling because he saw her before she saw him, Mohal sauntered up to Priya.

"I'm not late, am I?" he asked hopefully, looking up at the white clock face.

"Ha, ha, ha. If you are going to be late, don't meet by the Clock Tower!" Priya joked,

"It's a dead give away!"

They were both pleased to relieve their tension as they laughed while they strolled along Gallowtree Gate, past the brightly lit displays in the shop windows, until they were approaching Halford Street, where it had been reported that an Asian woman had been forced into a car on the day that Rita disappeared. Here, on the opposite corner to the Information Centre, was a branch of Caffe Nero, the one where Rita worked when back from Warwick University. Rita had said she needed the money. Her spell in Venice, part of her history course, was coming up soon and she wanted to earn funds for that. If she ever turned up, thought Priya, shaking her head as they navigated their way along the broad, pedestrianised, area to the café.

It was becoming the time of day when the town started to empty of elderly shoppers and fill up instead with students on their way home from school or college. These had a habit of herding together in intimidating groups, taking up swathes of the pavement, laughing and joking among themselves, chasing and cursing one another in colourful language. Their phones were ostentatiously part of this parade as group members took selfies, checked out pictures previously taken, or caught their friends in funny, embarrassing or awkward poses such as falling over a bin or hanging from a lamp post. Some were laughing at the discomfort of their fellows and planning further humiliation for the bus home.

"Were we ever like that?" Mohal asked Priya, looking

disdainfully at the teenagers who were scarcely much younger than his brother.

"Well I wasn't." Priya replied indignantly "But I can't speak for you!" she laughed as they went through the doorway.

Brother and friend were keen to check that Rita had done as she had planned and dropped in at the café on her way to meet Jacob, so putting herself in all likelihood as the figure of the abduction which the Big Issue seller had seen. Bruno, the manager, was behind the counter and waved to them, smiling through his well-tended beard.

"Leicester's only hipster!" Mohal whispered to Priya as they approached him.

Priya only half nodded, her gaze not focused on Bruno, but on the photo of Rita which was pinned in the middle of the notice board to his right. Beneath it was the text of the police appeal for information or witnesses. Mohal saw it too and touched his jacket pocket where he had stored more copies of the photograph in case they helped to jog people's memories. The family had conferred before agreeing on the picture of Rita which the police should use. Several possibilities put forward by Padma were vetoed by her sons to protect their sister. They doubted their mother's idea of how Rita would want the world to see her. "No way!" "Not that one" "Ugh! Gross!" had been their comments until a suitable photo was agreed on.

I don't suppose there's any news?" asked Bruno, bending from his great height like a tennis player at the net – he was six feet seven, Rita had told Priya. He set down two mugs of mint tea for them. "On the house." he said, and spread out his hands. Then he shook his head and grimaced beneath his black whiskers as if to empathise with their search.

What was it suddenly about men and beards? Seeing him reminded Priya that she and Rita had discussed this when they last spoke, on Facetime, a day before she went missing. "When did that happen?" Rita had said. Beards were fashionable and it was clean-shaven men like Mohal who suddenly looked like the exception. Priya had said she wondered if it was because growing a beard was one thing women could not - acceptably - do. After all, men were copying women in so many other ways these days – childcare, moisturiser, wearing their hair in buns. Rita had pointed out the effect of religion on appearance as well – she told Priya she was looking at the religious regimes during the Protectorate, which was established after the English Civil War, in her history course, and drawing comparisons with the attempts in the middle east to establish a caliphate with a strict dress and behavioural code. There was no doubt, Rita had told her, that the flamboyance and bright colours that pervaded in England after the restoration of the monarchy were in response to the dull colours and hues favoured by the Puritans during their years in power. Beards became very fashionable in that period too, Rita had said.

"No news" Mohal sighed.

"We thought we might try to jog some memories." Priya added. "It has been a few days since Rita was last seen. We wanted to check that she came in here that day?"

"Yeh. She did, apparently. Wish I'd been on shift then. But the police spoke to Maria and Gino who were here. Nothing odd happened. She was on her way to meet her boyfriend, I think they said?" Bruno tried to be helpful.

Priya and Mohal nodded. While Priya continued talking to Bruno, Mohal started to go around the tables with Rita's photo.

"She was here a few days ago. Did you see her? Do you remember her?" People were keen to help, but their heads were shaking.

"I did read about her in the paper." said a middle-aged man with grey hair and a short grey beard, donning reading glasses to examine the picture.

"She works here, sometimes doesn't she?" said his female

companion, showing herself to be a regular customer. She looked a bit younger than her friend. Her short sleeves revealed bare arms with mottled skin and she had the scratched voice of a smoker. "When was she here last?" she asked.

"Friday afternoon" Mohal confirmed.

"Then I did see her!" the woman sounded pleased she could help. "The young lady's phone wasn't working. Something about having no credit? I think she tried to make a call and it got cut off."

Mohal was nodding enthusiastically now. Here was a clue at last.

"So, she asked if she could borrow my phone." the woman continued.

"Really? You are sure it was her?" Mohal could hardly believe his luck.

"Yeh. She rang a number and left a message, I think. It didn't sound like a conversation – not that I was really listening- but more like she was talking to a voicemail." the customer confirmed.

"You don't know who she was calling? It could be important." Mohal pressed.

"Well no. But the number might still be in my phone, in the log." the customer started to take out her phone to look. Mohal was getting excited. It was all he could do not to snatch the phone from her and look himself. The woman seemed to be very slow at accessing the information.

"There!" finally she showed him the number which his sister had dialed.

* * *

Ten minutes later and Mohal was sitting at a table in the café opposite Priya. He had relayed to her the news about the phone call. Priya thought she recognized the number and, on checking her own phone, she turned out to be right. Rita had called a friend of theirs, Morwenna Maitland. Feeling like they really were following in Rita's steps, the pair had tried the number, but all they got was Morwenna's recorded message- "I must be doing something more interesting than talking to you! Speak after the beep."

Mohal rang the police number which the family had been given and, when his call was diverted, passed all this on to DC Gardner in a voicemail message. Was no one answering their phones anymore? he thought.

While they waited for Morwenna to get back to them, they finished their tea at the counter.

"So that's why her last call was made from here." Mohal said. "She ran out of credit so she couldn't even finish the call. She wouldn't have been able to ring out after that. Not until she had topped up her phone. I kept telling her to get one on contract, but she pleaded poverty and said as a student she couldn't afford it."

"But you don't know why she wanted to talk to this Morwenna?" Bruno asked, "She was going to meet the boyfriend, wasn't she? Jacob something. I never met him. Does Morwenna know him perhaps?" he speculated.

"She might. Jacob's an actor." Priya told Bruno. "We first met him when we worked at a bed and breakfast place run by Morwenna's mother, but, even if Morwenna remembers him, I doubt she knows him well. Morwenna is studying at Exeter Uni and, anyway, she doesn't take much interest in the bed and breakfast business. What we do know is that Rita was dressed to surprise Jacob for his birthday. But she never arrived."

"How was she getting to Jacob's? Did she have her car? What about CCTV?" Bruno asked.

"She told my brother that she was going by bus. Jacob had a car at the Coop where he worked. He would have dropped her back at home. At least I think that was her plan. But she's not on any CCTV. She just disappeared." Mohal explained, lifting his mug to finish the last of his tea.

"And did you find out?" Bruno asked almost casually as he wiped down the surface of the counter.

"Find out what?" Mohal said, pausing the mug on its way to his mouth.

"Whatever it was that she had remembered" Bruno amplified.

"What do you mean?" Priya spoke this time.

"Surely you know?" Bruno was incredulous. He went on "She told Gino that she'd remembered something else about that day, the day when that dead man fell out of the train on top of her. Maybe that's what she wanted to discuss with Morwenna. Don't you know what it was?".

Chapter

8

"If you love someone then tell them right away; because after missing the train there is no use of yelling that you had a ticket"

Wrushank Sorte

Wednesday 27th April 2016 3pm
5 days missing

Priya and Mohal left Caffe Nero in thoughtful mood. What was it that Rita had remembered? Who had she told? What was it that she wanted to talk to Morwenna about? Did it have any bearing on her disappearance? Setting off for Mohal's car , they had to cross Halford Street and neither of them could prevent their glances from turning to their left to see the spot where the woman had reportedly been abducted. There was nothing unusual to see, nothing to suggest their sister and friend had been forced into a car there.

As the pair walked along Granby Street, Mohal gave out a few more copies of Rita's picture to bewildered passers-by. "Did you see her?" "Do you remember her?" Some avoided the two of them, thinking they were selling something or handing out referendum literature. Some shook their heads or shrugged their shoulders, others nodded in understanding – they had seen reports of Rita's disappearance on the local news or heard about it on Twitter and other social media. But no one had anything to tell them.

Reaching the corner of Granby Street and Rutland Street they saw a Big Issuer seller. He was white and his appearance, made ragged by experiences of homelessness, made his age hard to guess. The seller's long grey hair was tied together at

41

the back of his neck with a piece of string. He had a dusting of stubble, like white sand paper, above his upper lip and across his chin. At his feet sat a dog of mixed parentage; it had a lean body, like a greyhound, and was coloured white, black and brown in various places. While the man was animated "Help the homeless! Buy a Big Issue!" the dog was listless and his long face and large eyes made him look sad.

Perhaps the dog was just bored, thought Priya as she and Mohal approached.

"Here you go" Mohal proffered some coins to the vendor. "Been on this corner long?" he asked as Priya bent to stroke the dog, who perked up at the attention and wagged his tail.

"Just this week." the man replied in a local accent, "We change our pitches regular like. Some are better than others."

"OK" Mohal said slowly. "We're trying to find out what happened to my sister." He showed the seller the picture of Rita.

"Oh yeh" said the man, pausing to yell "Big Issue! Help the Homeless! Someone buy the last one!" and to receive some change from a passing shopper "Oh, ta duck" he said.

The seller turned his attention back to the photo. "Yeh. I heard some talk about 'er. That she were missing, like." the seller said, looking down at Priya who was standing up again after fussing over the dog.

"Apparently one of the sellers may have seen something?" Priya addressed the man. "They may have seen a woman being forced into a car?"

The man was shaking his head.

"You don't know which seller that was,by any chance?" Mohal put in, "The police won't tell us".

Somewhere behind the man's eyes something registered. "Oh, I see. Mebbe they don't want to get involved. Can't say as I blame them." He looked around him, hopeful for more trade possibilities, although the number of people on the streets was diminishing. "Time to pack up soon. Not many punters out 'ere now."

"No" Mohal sympathised.

"What's the best pitch?" Priya asked.

"Town 'All Square" the man replied, "W'out a doubt. Lots of punters there. Come to think of it.." he stopped a moment, a thought descending into his brain like a coin dropping into a machine. "You prob'ly want to go there now. Talk to Nadiya. She can prob'ly 'elp you. Big Issue! Big Issue!" he shouted as he made clear their audience with him was over.

"Cheers, mate" Mohal said as they moved away and Priya waved goodbye to the man and the dog.

"Do you think Nadiya is the witness?" Priya asked as they retraced their steps and then turned from the mainly glass facades of the shops on Granby Street to the older and more elegantly built brick buildings on Bishop Street, one of the thoroughfares flanking the square over which the town hall building, dating to 1875, presided.

"Let's hope so." Mohal replied.

* * *

At first there was no sign of a Big Issue seller. When they arrived at the elegant Queen Anne style town hall building, the square in front of it, guarded by bronzed lions around a fountain, was being criss-crossed by workers and shoppers hurrying home and using it as a pleasant short cut. A few teenagers were sitting on one of the benches. Two elderly Asian men sat together on another bench, their walking sticks held in front of them. Although talking together, their heads were bowed and their comments were addressed to the ground. They were too far away to be heard, but their gestures suggested they were less than impressed with the teenagers' behaviour.

Then Priya saw her. She was a young woman enveloped in a brown tunic and wearing an orange hijab which covered her head and flowed down her neck and across her chest. Over her tunic she wore the ubiquitous red waist coat of a Big Issuer seller. She was crouched on the ground, propped up by a tree trunk. Where the previous seller had been animated and lively, she was gave an overall impression of weariness. The pair walked up to her slowly, as if she were a shy deer who they might frighten off by sudden movements.

"Hello" Priya took the initiative, crouching low, just as she had earlier on to fuss over the dog. "I'll take one of those" and she prised a copy of the magazine from the young woman's grip while putting some coins into her other gloved hand.

"Been here long?" Priya continued, while Mohal kept his distance and watched the antics of the teenagers who were jumping on and off the bench now, their school rucksacks on the ground, forgotten.

"Only this afternoon. I am not well." the seller sighed and put her hands in her lap.

"It's a good spot though?" Priya asked.

"Yeh.Pretty good. I don't have many left" the vendor replied, showing Priya the small pile of magazines in her hand.

"That's good. Nadiya isn't it?" When she saw the startled look on the woman's face Priya hastily added "We talked to the seller on Granby Street, He said that was your name."

"Charlie. You saw Charlie. He is nice. He looks out for me." The young woman raised her gaze to look at Priya for the first time.

"That's good" Priya nodded. "We were speaking to him because we are concerned about my friend – his sister.." she pointed at Mohal, "We don't know where she's gone. The police said a Big Issuer seller had come forward with some possible information." As she spoke, Priya held out a copy of Rita's photo.

At first the young woman seemed uninterested. She looked away again and started to pull at the grass around the base of the tree. Then she sighed as if a decision had been made and turned to look at Priya.

"Yes. Was me. I can't be sure it was your sister…" Priya did not correct her mistake, better to wait and see what information Nadiya could provide.

"On Friday, I was on Granby Street, where Charlie is today. I was sitting on the ground at the corner with Halford Street, near the cafe. I can't stand all day. My legs suffer. I wasn't paying attention. I get bored, you know?" Priya nodded understanding.

"There were cars, always cars! Then this one, I don't know about cars but it was white colour I think, or maybe silver, and a woman in a blue sari. I noticed the sari, lovely material, and I don't think she wanted to get in the car… I don't know.. just a feeling, you know?" Again, Priya nodded. "Two, no, maybe three men. One driving and one or two in the back with her. Hard to say."

"Do you remember anything about the men?" Priya asked, noticing that Mohal had drawn closer to catch what Nadiya had to say.

"Not much. Too far. Eyes not good!" Nadiya smiled apologetically. "Young, I think. Like football players. One was black, one maybe Asian." she added. "Sorry" she shrugged, "That's all I know. Don't want no trouble." she added nervously.

"Oh no!" Priya tried to sound reassuring. "We won't tell anyone who you are. Thanks for talking to us." she said as she put some extra money into the young woman's gloved fingers before they left the Square.

* * *

"It sounds like Rita, then" Mohal broke the silence between them as they walked to his car. Mohal had taken the opportunity to put up a few copies of Rita's photo on the trees around the square. So many people passed through, maybe one of them would remember something? He had written, "MISSING. Please call.." and left his mobile number. It was a long shot but you never knew.

"Yeh. The sari is too much of a coincidence." Priya agreed.

"Good job she was wearing it." Mohal put in, trying to lift their mutual mood. "Nadiya might not have noticed otherwise."

"Yeh" Priya replied, "But I don't like to think of it. Who took Rita? Why? What do they want? It just doesn't look good. There's been no word. It can only be that they meant her harm." and Priya stopped in the street for a moment, unable to walk on at the thought of what might have happened to her friend.

"Hey" Mohal put a reassuring arm round the shoulders of his sister's friend. "It'll be OK. Rita's a tough nut. We'll find her." Priya nodded and pressed her lips together in determination.

"You're right. Let's go see what Jacob has to say." she said.

* * *

There was no sign of Rita's boyfriend when they reached the store in Wigston, a town south of Leicester, not far from Oadby where Rita's family home was, and a short drive from the town centre. A large woman was on the till at the Coop, her substantial arms reaching forward for the goods to scan, her broad shoulders easily able to pack bags for the mainly elderly customers and help them put their purchases into their shopping trolleys. A man wearing a black fleece over a shirt and tie was on the floor near the till, stacking a shelf of canned vegetables; he wore a green badge declaring him to be the manager. He had a short dark beard growing close around the contours of his chin and his hair was thick on the top of his head and shaved at the sides.

"Excuse me, we're looking for Jacob? It's about his missing girlfriend?" and once again Mohal produced the photo of Rita.

The shelf stacker stood up. "Oh yeh. Jacob is really cut up about all this." he said, looking at the picture of Rita. "I'm the manager here." He pointed to his badge as if they needed evidence.

"I was on duty on Friday – the day they say that Miss Patel was coming here. But she didn't. Jacob was doing a shift." the manager stared into the distance as if to help his memory. "We are open until eight every day except Sunday." He added inconsequentially. "I think maybe he half expected to see her. He was agitated all day. I caught him on his phone several times." The manager's hands were animated as he spoke, as if that also helped him recall that day. "In the end, I told Jacob to go home early. He just wasn't concentrating. I think he must have met up with some mates that evening. He got in late the next day and was very much the worse for wear. Then the police came to see him to say Rita was missing and he hasn't been himself since." He stopped for a moment, "I don't know, actors!" he added, throwing up his hands dramatically. "More trouble than they're worth sometimes! But I guess Jacob has a lot to worry about at the moment. I hope they find the girl soon."

"Thanks" Mohal said. "Rita's my sister. We just can't think what happened to her."

"Well, you have my sympathy. It must be a great worry. Jacob's out there. Go on through." The manager pointed to a door at the back of the shop. Priya and Mohal followed his directions.

Jacob wasn't in the storage area where they found themselves and, in answer to their inquiry, a young man with spiky blond hair and a ring in his nose, who was applying a brush to the floor, pointed towards the delivery bay and car park at the back. They passed through a curtain of plastic strips to find a tarmacked area where three cars were parked at one end. Jacob could be seen inside one of them, on the driver's side of a white Peugeot. He seemed to be multitasking, simultaneously wiping down the dash board while talking animatedly on his phone. Mohal waved to attract his attention and he appeared to end his call before opening the car door and stepping out. He wore a baseball cap on his head of dreadlocks, the peak peering down his neck, the back of the hat clinging to his forehead. He was wearing a black shirt over black jeans and carefully stepped into the pool of water he had created next to the car in his brown boots.

"Hi" Jacob lifted a friendly hand in greeting, his dark shirt rolled to the elbows showing well-toned arm muscles. "I think I recognize you. Rita's brother?" Mohal nodded.

"Yeh. I kinda recognise you from pictures she showed me. Mohan, right?" he attempted.

"Mohal" he confirmed, "and our younger brother is Nayan."

"Yeh, I get it now. Any news of Rita? I have to say I've been going out of my mind bro."

As Jacob shook his head, his dreadlocks shivered. "I just don't know what to think, man." he added, looking doleful, like a lost puppy. "And how are you doing Priya?" He bent to take up her hand and kissed it on the back theatrically.

"The manager said you would be in the storage bay." Priya replied in her firm voice, one she had been practising with potentially flirtatious patients on her ward round training.

"We're expecting a delivery any time" Jacob explained. "I was just cleaning my car while I wait. It's easier to do here than outside the house where I live."

"Do you usually drive here? Did you have the car here on your birthday for example?" Priya thought Mohal's voice sounded rather sharp when he spoke and she noticed his eyes narrowing.

"No, I didn't, actually." Jacob didn't seem to realise he was being accused. "I thought I would have a skinful at some point, so better to leave the car at home."

"Oh. So what time did you leave here, on Friday, on your birthday?" was Mohal's next question.

"I don't know exactly. Eddie, that's the manager, let me go early. It was after the 3pm delivery had arrived and been stacked. I wanted to speak to Rita, but she wasn't picking up. I left several messages. It got worse on the bus home. Her phone was switched off altogether. I thought she'd blown me out, or that she'd forgotten. When I got back to the house I share, I met a friend and we were in the pub all night, just lots of beers and then a curry. I left my phone on but Rita never called."

"And you didn't try any of us? Her family or her friends? To see where she was?" Priya wanted to know.

"Well, I didn't know she was missing, did I? I didn't know she was planning to surprise me. There wasn't any reason to be concerned. And I didn't have your numbers. She kept us very much apart you know." Jacob sounded a little embarrassed now. Priya and Mohal nodded to one another in acknowledgement. It was true. Although they knew that Rita was seeing Jacob, she never invited him to join in anything her family or friends were doing. She seemed to want that part of her life to be separate. Perhaps this explained why he had seemed so distant on social media – he hadn't joined in any of the on-line discussions about Rita's whereabouts, which Priya had found strange.

"Did she say much to you about the trial?" Priya tried a different approach. "According to Bruno at Caffe Nero, Rita thought she might have remembered something significant. He thought she was going to tell someone?" she continued.

"Yeh, when the police came to see me, they mentioned the train murder and the trial. They said they thought there might be a connection. Rita and I skyped the day before she disappeared and she did say something…"

"Well?" Mohal was pleased to hear the police had questioned Jacob, but was starting to losing patience now. What was the matter with the guy? Didn't he know how important this was? he was thinking.

"I didn't pay much attention to be honest. She was always chatterin' on about somethin'." Jacob replied languidly. For a man who liked to perform before an audience, Jacob did not seem to appreciate his questioners' keen anticipation for his answers.

Priya was also getting annoyed with this. Jacob seemed very self-absorbed. If only he had paid attention to her friend!

Finally, Jacob raised his eyebrows and put a finger to his forehead signaling that he had just had a thought. "Something about a coat not being a coat? But she wasn't sure if it was the barristers in court who had put the idea in her head. She couldn't sort out what was in her memory and what she might have imagined afterwards."

"And did you tell the police this?" Mohal wanted to know.

"No. I don't think so." Jacob looked perplexed. "I don't think they asked. Well I didn't think it was important. Do you think it might be?"

Chapter

9

"When you are on a railway station platform waiting for the train that is due, and when you come to know that it arrives five hours late, how do you react? You fling abusive words at train."

Sri Sathya Sai Baba

Wednesday 27th April 2016 5pm
5 days missing

"Come on! Come on! Pick up!" Sitting in Mohal's car, a silver Golf he had purchased after a pay rise at work, Priya sighed as Morwenna Maitland failed once again to answer her phone. "Morwenna, call me as soon as you get this, yeh? It's Priya. It's important."

Priya sighed with frustration. "Another dead end! How will we ever find her?" Despair cracked her voice.

"We will." Mohal tried to sound positive "That coat business might be an important clue."

"I just wish Morwenna would call me back." Priya stared at her phone as if she could will it to ring.

"How else will we know what Rita wanted to talk to her about?" she asked, not expecting a reply.

Mohal had an idea "We can call on Athena if you like." he offered, knowing that Priya would be pleased to have an excuse to extend their investigations and visit Morwenna's mother, an old friend.

"At least it's a plan" Priya sighed again. The effect was less enthusiastic than Mohal had been hoping for. Then her face brightened. "Yes, let's do that." She rewarded him with a smile at last and he selected the route on his sat nav.

Mohal joined the traffic snaking its way around the circumference of the City, the cars crawling between sets of traffic lights as if they themselves were weary from a day's work. There was a lot of traffic on the other side of the ring road, trying to escape from the city, and they got held up at various junctions, especially when it came to crossing Aylestone Lane on their way to the Knighton district of the city where the bed and breakfast business run by Athena Maitland was situated.

"I hope she's in." Priya spoke as their car was able to cross the junction at last. She was starting to have doubts about their intentions now.

"She will be" Mohal found himself providing reassurance again. "Rita used to say the evening was a busy time for the business. People who have booked arrive and some guests just turn up on spec.'Walk-ins' she called them. Doesn't Athena sometimes cook soup for them as well?"

"Yes, she does." Priya smiled at the memory. She could almost smell the aroma of the vegetable soups which Athena liked to prepare. "She enjoys making them food, even though it's supposed to be only breakfast she provides" Priya had a picture in her mind now of confident, assured, Athena with her glossy auburn hair competently answering the queries and seeing to the demands of her guests. However busy, she had always checked that she and Rita were coping with their cleaning work and provided a listening ear for their problems. Morwenna had no idea how lucky she was to have a mother like that, thought Priya, whose own mother ran a clothing business from home and always seemed preoccupied with it. Morwenna seemed to glide through life unaware of how fortunate she was. Which was another reason why it was exasperating that she would not answer her phone! Maybe Athena could explain what was going on.

Nearing the B&B, Priya was looking out of the car window at large houses at the end of long driveways; most had been converted into student accommodation to meet the expanding needs of Leicester University. Of course, the city had two Universities to accommodate, didn't it, Priya reminded herself; wasn't Rita's brother, Nayan, hoping to go to one of them, De Montfort? She must check with Rita when…Priya stopped her train of thought. There was no point feeling sorry for herself over her missing friend, it was time to take some action.

Athena and her husband, Edward, had converted their house into a business some years ago to provide income to meet their daughter's school fees. Edward, a lawyer specialising in intellectual property, spent a lot of time abroad, leaving Athena to run the place. Morwenna was now away most of the time too, studying at Exeter University, but, Priya thought, to be honest, she had not contributed much to the workforce when she was around. During the time that Priya and Rita had spent working at Sundial in the holidays, they had seen Morwenna infrequently and usually only when she wanted something from the kitchen. An English student, Morwenna had often seemed to Priya as if she had her head in the clouds. Priya wondered what sort of career path she would eventually follow. Perhaps she would take up acting, like so many of her group of friends seemed to be intent on doing, from what Priya had gleaned on Facebook, or perhaps she would work in publishing or public relations. It was likely to be something to do with people, Priya thought, and probably to require a lot of business lunches and parties. Morwenna revelled in social occasions and liked to be the centre of attention. Rita, on the other hand, took an interest in other people and seemed to notice everything going on around her, hence her interest in solving mysteries about them. So, it was hard to think that her friend had wanted to pick Morwenna's brains about something. What could it have been?

There was one parking space left at the front of the house,

where cars gathered around the central sundial, after which the guest house was named. This suggested that business was good, Priya thought, and her hopes of finding Athena at home rose. Given the time of day, the pair decided to try the main door first, rather than to ring the bell for Athena's basement flat.

To their surprise, the door was opened almost immediately. The pair were further taken aback when they took in the appearance of Athena, who was standing in the open doorway to welcome them. She wore skinny jeans and a black T-shirt with a visible rip in one of the shoulders; the clothes were unusually casual for her, and her face was a bit pinched, in fact she looked like she might have lost some weight. But the most striking aspect of her appearance was her hair. The auburn tresses had been replaced by a short bob, the nearest colour to which one would have to call purple, Priya thought, closing her bottom jaw to meet the top as her mouth had slid open in surprise.

"Oh, hello you two." Athena sounded brisk, "Come on in." she said as if she had been expecting them.

They followed Athena into the hall and, crossing the black and white tiled floor, entered the kitchen where, as they had suspected, Athena had a pan of soup on the hob.

"Smells good!" Mohal ventured.

"Leek and potato." Athena replied. "Can I get you a drink? Or you can have some soup if you like. I am just waiting for one more guest to arrive." Athena was business-like rather than welcoming, as if they were just another chore on her list.

"Oh, we haven't come to get in the way." Priya reassured her. "We've been trying to contact Morwenna but she's not answering her phone."

Athena seemed to crumple a little at this and sat on one of the chairs by the pine table, gesturing to Priya and Mohal to do the same. She poured them all water from a glass jug which sat on a wicker mat in the centre of the table.

"Oh, I'm sorry." Athena shook her head. Now they were sitting down Priya could also see that Athena had several piercings in her ears through which she wore various gold and silver slivers that looked like tiny daggers. This was uncharacteristic of her as well, Priya thought. What was going on?

"You must be concerned about your sister." Athena had turned to Mohal. "Is there any news? Morwenna told me she had gone missing."

"No developments." Mohal confirmed. "It seems likely she was bundled into a car…"

"No!" Athena put her hand to her mouth in shock. Mohal had got so used to the idea by now that he had forgotten the effect the information might have on other people when they heard it for the first time.

"We think it was Rita. Anyway, the thing is, we found out today that just before she disappeared, or was taken, or whatever, she tried to make a call, to ring Morwenna." he paused to sip some of the water.

"Oh!" Athena was surprised. "Well I don't know if I can help you. I don't know what is happening to my family at all at the moment!". Athena's hand shook as she raised her own glass to her mouth.

"What's wrong?" Priya instinctively asked her friend to explain, putting aside thoughts of the mission with which they had arrived at Sundial.

"Oh, I don't know!" Athena's tone was petulant and her voice too loud. She spoke like someone slightly drunk, although there were no signs that she had actually been drinking. "What could be wrong, apart from that my husband is having an affair and doesn't care if I know it! Morwenna has stopped answering her phone so she doesn't have to speak to either of us. She is very upset about it all!" Athena put her head in her hands, then shook herself and looked up.

"It's all a mess!" she said despairingly. "I can't imagine what Edward was thinking of. He certainly wasn't thinking of the consequences!"

Mohal and Priya looked at each other questioningly. An upset Athena was not what they had expected. She usually provided the comfort rather than sought it. Would she be any help to them now?

"I don't think he would want to hurt you." Mohal tried. He had not met Edward Maitland very often, and when their paths had crossed it had been briefly, usually when Mohal was picking up his sister after her work was finished. They had exchanged formalities and talked about trivialities. But Mohal felt he should try to put in a good word for the male gender.

"Oh, I don't think he meant anything!" Athena was dismissive. "I think he just did what he wanted at the time. He didn't think what it meant to me, or to Morwenna, or for our life here." Athena gestured around the kitchen, as if its pots and pans, plates and cutlery, were items that should have been uppermost in her wandering husband's mind.

"But there we are!" she sighed deeply and finished her drink of water. "It does have a meaning. It means we shall probably have to sell this place. And I shall have to decide what I want to do next, and where I want to do it!"

"Really?" Priya was aghast. How could this have been going on and neither she nor Rita knew about it? "You don't think you can be reconciled?" she tried.

"Oh no!" Athena shook her head quickly, causing tremors in the little daggers in her ears. "I can't be second best. I think he always knew that. That's why he tried to keep it a secret from me, from Morwenna too."

"Oh dear." Priya was sympathetic.

"Morwenna has taken it badly then?" Mohal put in, hoping to get the conversation back to the subject he was interested in-the phone call his sister had made before she vanished.

"Yes. She's gone to London to stay with some friends from University. For some reason, they all seem to end up living in the East End, near the Olympic Games site. I don't know why. But I can call her and tell her you need her help. I am sure she would want to do everything she can if it is for Rita, Rita was very good to her when she got herself in a bit of a fix." Athena was standing now and taking her phone from the dresser in the corner of the kitchen.

"Hello Morwenna. Mum here. I've got Priya and Mohal with me. They very much want to speak to you, my darling. You might be able to help with where poor Rita is. Please say you will talk to them, my love." She added to her daughter's collection of voicemails.

* * *

Mohal drove Priya back to her parents' house in Loughborough. As they took the A6, passing through the town of Rothley and Quorn village, both agreed it was fitting that they return to the 'scene of the crime' as Mohal called it, meaning the town where Rita had managed to get herself involved in yet another dead body mystery the previous summer. They discussed Athena's bedraggled appearance and her surprising news.

"No wonder Morwenna is not taking any calls! Everything is changing for her. She must be very confused." Priya said. Mohal coughed sceptically. Privately he thought Morwenna was behaving selfishly. He remembered how hard he and his brother and sister had tried to help their mother through the grief of their father's sudden death last year. They had not gone away and shut themselves off from the world.

"At least we got her to agree to speak to us." was all he replied.

As a result of her mother's call, Morwenna had texted

and promised to Facetime Priya in an hour. So, brother and friend were on a quest to reach Loughborough in time to catch Morwenna on Priya's iPad.

"Ah Priya!" Mrs. Shah beamed as her daughter arrived home with Rita's brother in tow. She had always had a soft spot for Mohal, "Such a nice boy and hard working too", she would say to her daughter. Appearances can be deceptive Priya was tempted to reply but never did.

"I wondered if you would be back for supper, I was thinking…" but Mrs. Shah's thoughts would have to remain in her head as, disconcertingly, Priya dashed past her and up the stairs, dragging Mohal behind her urgently.

"Later, Mum!" Priya called from the top of the stairs and Mohal glanced back apologetically before being pulled into Priya's room, followed by the door being firmly closed.

"Well!" Mrs. Shah shook her head indignantly and took herself off to the solace of her kitchen and Classic FM.

"Hi both!" Morwenna's face looked unnaturally round as she appeared on the screen; she was leaning in too close. When she sat back on her chair, satisfied the three of them were connected, her natural good looks were apparent; her long fair hair framed a smooth complexion and her eyes were glittering beneath smoky eye shadow and the latest trend in heavily drawn-in eyebrows. If she didn't know better, Priya would suspect the young woman had applied her make up especially before making the call. Priya smoothed down her own dark locks with her hands as they spoke.

"Any news on Rita?" Morwenna asked before either Priya or Mohal could speak. They were sitting together on the edge of Priya's bed, her iPad propped up opposite them on her desk.

"'Fraid not" Mohal shook his head. "We've been in the city centre today, trying to jog people's memories." he told Morwenna, not wanting to sound as if nothing was happening.

"It must be petrifying!" Morwenna was not given to understatement, "I dread to think what she might be going through!"

Priya was getting alarmed now. Neither she nor Mohal needed to dwell on Rita's possible fate. They wanted to stay positive.

"Well, we just don't know do we?" she ventured. "But we thought you might be able to help."

"I can't think how, but try me." Morwenna rubbed her manicured hands together to show enthusiasm.

"We think maybe Rita's disappearance is somehow connected to the trial, you know, when she gave evidence about that body that fell on top of her when she opened the train door.." Mohal tried to make their request sound coherent, but felt he was failing.

"Mmmn?" Morwenna was wearing a puzzled expression. Where was this going? she wondered.

"It seems that Rita remembered something, something to do with her evidence. Jacob, her boyfriend, told us he thought that Rita was going to talk to you. So, we wanted to know whether she did, speak to you I mean, maybe before she disappeared?"

"OMG!" Morwenna put her hand to her mouth as if to suppress further imprecations.

"She did call me, on the phone, but I never thought, that is to say I never imagined…" Morwenna was not making much sense.

"What?" Mohal could bear it no longer, "What was it she wanted to talk about?"

"Well, memory really" Morwenna gave an unexpected reply.

"Memory?" Priya echoed disbelievingly.

"Yeh" Morwenna nodded as if this was self-explanatory.

"Meaning?" Mohal prompted. Then, as Morwenna seemed not to realise she had not made herself clear, he added, "What was it about memory that she wanted to discuss?" he asked.

"Well, about when something bad has happened – and you know what a horrible situation I got caught up in - well, whether the shock sort of shuts off your memory and whether, later, after a bit of time, your memories came back. Or whether, maybe, the shock meant your memories were distorted and not real."

"Okay" Mohal spoke slowly, trying to understand, "And which was it, in your opinion?"

"Which was what?" Morwenna was looking puzzled.

"Did you say you thought that genuine memories could come back, or that anything you thought you remembered couldn't be relied on?"

"Neither" said Morwenna mystifyingly.

"Neither?" Priya took up the questioning.

"Yeh. We got cut off. I think she ran out of credit. I tried to call her back, but first her phone was engaged and after that I couldn't get any answer at all. Her number was not recognised. While I was calling her, she must have been calling me from another phone because I got a voicemail. She just said sorry and she would call later. I didn't hear from her after that."

"Oh great!" Mohal threw his hands up in exasperation. Another dead end, he was thinking. Priya gave him a warning glance. It was not Morwenna's fault if Rita's call had not helped them work out where she was now.

"And this was when, exactly?" Priya queried, twisting strands of her hair between her fingers as she spoke.

"Well, I guess it was the day she disappeared. Last Friday. I did leave a message with the police, to let them know. I don't know if they think it was important. They haven't got back to me."

"Priya!" Mrs. Shah's voice was coming up the stairs now. She had sat through the Albinoni adagio and the duet from the Pearl Fishers before her patience had become exhausted. "Are you going to be very much longer?"

Priya raised her eyes to the ceiling. "Won't be long." she said and left the room to converse with her parent while Mohal tried to continue the conversation with Morwenna. He wasn't sure what to say exactly. He didn't want to upset her or add to her alarm.

"Do you have memories?" he settled on, "Details you remember now, that you didn't remember when you got caught up in things."

"Oh yeh" Morwenna was quite open about it. "That's what I would have told Rita. You do recall things later. And they are valid. It's as if your brain protects you at first, stops you thinking about all of it. Then little bits come back. When your brain thinks it can cope."

"And they are valid memories?" Mohal probed. As well as hoping to promote the search for his sister, he was interested as a journalist.

"I think so, yeh. Of course, it's difficult when there has been lots of information in the media. But I really think you know what has come from your head and what has come from someone else's experience. You can feel it, sort of smell it, you know?" she smiled from the screen.

"I think I get it." Mohal nodded. "Perhaps my sister was on to something real, something that might have made a difference to the police case."

"Yeh" Morwenna agreed, "But if she did, is that what got her into trouble? And what kind of trouble? It's doing my head in thinking about it."

Chapter

10

"Sir, Sunday morning, although recurring at regular and well foreseen intervals, always seems to take this railway by surprise."

W S Gilbert

Sunday 1ˢᵗ May 2016 3am
9 days missing

David Hann was asleep when the call came. He stirred next to his wife and reached for his phone. Seeing a work number, he managed to mutter "DS Hann" as he struggled to escape from the bed clothes and pad his way to their en suite bathroom. Catching sight in the mirror of his puffy face and untidy hair, he decided it was no time to confront his appearance and turned away to face the door he had closed behind him.

"Sorry to wake you, sir" a Constable said. "But a body has been found. We thought you'd want to know."

"Female?" the Sergeant was trying to shake himself to full consciousness, guessing what this was about.

"Young, Asian, fits the profile for Rita Patel, sir. She's wearing a sari. Hard to tell what colour it is" came the unwelcome answer.

"Why? Where was she?" David Hann knew he would have to get all the details but he wanted a quick overview so he could paint the scene and see if he thought he could envisage Rita fitting into it.

"She was in the river Soar, near the Braunstone Gate Bridge." the Constable told him, naming a familiar landmark. "A member of the public going home after a night out saw her from the tow path."

"Hmmn" Sergeant Hann was worried now.

He thought the river might have some religious significance. He vaguely remembered reading that the council had designated a spot on the Soar where the City's Hindu, Jain and Sikh communities could scatter their loved ones' ashes, in order to avoid the cost and other difficulties of getting the ashes to the Ganges in India. He didn't think that place was near the Braunstone Gate Bridge. Still, it was troubling.

"Cause of death?" Hann hated to ask. He didn't want this to be Rita and he really didn't want to know what had happened to her if that was how their search ended, after all their efforts, after all the hope they had maintained.

"Unclear at the moment. The Medical Officer is attending now, to supervise the moving of the.." the Constable hesitated, realising that for DS Hann this was a sensitive case, "body" he said after a pause, unable to think of a better word. "Nothing obvious at the scene so far. It looks like she may have jumped in, possibly from the bridge?"

Detective Sergeant Hann sighed. Oh Rita! Surely you didn't! Of all the possible outcomes, suicide had barely entered his thoughts. David Hann had been on a training course recently concerning suspects with mental health issues. The module covered what signs to look for, how to arrest an agitated person if you suspected such problems, and the shortage of places where such persons could be held. The course included the increase in depression among what the trainers called 'millenials'. There seemed to be no one theory that was accepted as to why this was happening, although social media and on-line bullying were held up as possible culprits. But surely none of that applied to Rita Patel? By all accounts she was happy and busy, a determined person, a young woman with a purpose and everything to live for.

"OK" he almost groaned. "I'm on my way. I'll speak to the

DI and come to the scene. We need to get an ID as soon as we can. Meanwhile keep a lid on it. We need a news blackout 'til we have more information. We don't want to alarm the family unnecessarily and I am certainly not going to disturb their sleep with speculation. I assume the station are checking missing persons to see if the body matches anyone else?"

"Yes, sir, understood." was the Constable's short reply.

The call ended. The Sergeant returned to the bedroom to disturb his wife again.

"Put the light on!" she muttered from under the duvet. "I can't bear to hear you stumbling about in the dark. I guess you have to go out?"

"Sorry" David Hann crossed to the bed, "Ouch!" he stubbed his toe on the way to the lamp switch.

"I dread to think what you are like on surveillance!" his wife said through gritted teeth.

"A body has been found!" he told her as he pulled on his jeans and found a sweatshirt.

"I don't really wan to know!" she replied unsympathetically, turning her body encased in the duvet away from his and moving her head further below the bedcovers. "Just get on with it." she added, and then, "And if you do get back before seven can you sleep on the sofa?" she pleaded "I've got a difficult meeting tomorrow and I'd like to get some sleep. Somehow my boss doesn't appreciate what it's like to be married to a police officer!"

"Sure" DS Hann bent over the bed as he left the room, switching off the lamp and bestowing a kiss roughly where he thought his wife's head might be, although he could only vaguely make out a few tufts of her short black hair on the edge of the pillow.

In the car, the DS was able to talk hands free as he drove. First, he got an update from a Constable at the scene. The Medical Officer was too busy with the body to speak to him. She said she thought the body looked swollen but could not tell whether this was owing to its presence in the water or some other cause. Hann wasn't sure whether this was a good sign or not as regards his own investigation. He called DI Foster next. She seemed to wake very quickly and asked pertinent questions about identification almost before DS Hann could explain the situation.

"Get a photo to Inspector Bridge" Sue Foster told him. "He can save us and the family a lot of trouble if it's not Rita, and if it is…" she let the end of that sentence hang in the air between them. At least we will know what we are dealing with thought Hann, taking the turning for Hinkley. You had to be careful on this road, even at the dead of night he thought. Idiots would try to overtake at the most unsuitable places and the stretches of dual carriageway seemed to encourage some to try speeding to get past slow vehicles before they ended. The darkness and lack of vehicles brought out the drunks and the careless.

Hann decided not to disturb the other DI yet. He would wait until they had a good picture before he did so. Disturbing two Inspectors in one night was not something he relished. So, while he kept his eyes open for mad or bad drivers, he called the Constable again and arranged for a photo of the body to be sent to his phone.

As he neared the bridge a 'ping' sound told him the picture had arrived. He pulled into a layby, put on the car's interior light, and with trembling fingers scrolled to the picture and opened it up. He let out an exasperated breath when he saw the image. Dead people never looked like themselves, did they? They were like wax work versions of the person they had been. There was no doubting that their spirit had gone. This body was confusing. Yes, it was a young Asian woman. Yes, she had long hair. The hair colour and the shade of the clothes were hard to discern. The Constable had sent a couple of images, one concentrating on the face, the other on the overall appearance of the body. Both had suffered from immersion in what looked like pretty muddy water. A localised storm the previous evening had probably churned it up. Everything was bathed in a brown glaze, like a sepia photograph. The person's eyes were closed, mercifully. Hann wasn't sure he could have coped at that hour of the day if the body had been staring up at him from his phone screen. He reached into the glove pocket of his car and took a swig from the water bottle he kept there while he gave himself time to think.

Was this Rita? Did it resemble the photographs he had seen? Not having met the young woman he could not be sure. DC Gardner would be better at this he thought. She had at least met Rita in real life. She might have an instinct about this body; she might recognise Rita, or not. With a heavy heart, he realised that he could not make the decision. It was time to wake another Inspector. How to make yourself super unpopular in one night, he thought.

Sunday 1st May 2016 6am

Priya had not slept. Back in Oxford, she had gone to a party which started around midnight and went on all night, with dancing and revelry which got wilder as the hours progressed, in a group of college function rooms overlooking the river, with music thumping into the darkness. Many of her friends were the worse for drink by now, and wilting over bannisters and stairs on their way to get some fresh air, but as a non-drinker Priya was simply starting to feel tired. She had walked a little by the side of the river Cherwell, watching with amusement and a little horror as two students attempted to swim across the width of it. Prevented from jumping from Magdalen Bridge on May Day now, the undergraduates seemed to need to find another outlet for their high spirits. Back in the High by Magdalen tower, she joined friends pressed together in the crowd to hear the choir do their traditional singing, after which there would be breakfasts around the town, students in evening dress mingling with workers on their way to their places of business and ordinary folk in relaxed clothes. Priya was looking up at the tower, tears coming to her eyes as she recalled a conversation with Rita. Her friend had told her that during the English Civil War Charles I had stood at the top of that tower to watch the Parliamentary troops on manoeuvres up on the hill in nearby Headington. She hoped Rita was all right, wherever she was now.

Just as the choir was finishing, Priya's phone gave a beep. She looked down to see a text from a friend in Leicester. "Don't want to worry you but local news is saying a body of a woman has been found in the river Soar- hope it's not Rita?". All thoughts of breakfast were banished from Priya's mind as she tried in vain to move among the herd of people and find a way out. She needed to get access to more accurate news.

Sunday 1ˢᵗ May 2016 10 am

By morning, DS Hann, fuelled by coffee and an egg McMuffin from McDonalds, his home and bed a distant memory, was in the briefing meeting, waiting for the arrival of DI Sue Foster. He had kept her informed of developments as they unfolded during the night. She seemed able to cat nap successfully between his calls so that when she breezed in she looked as refreshed and ready for work as he looked crumpled and ready to rest.

Once he had splashed some cold water on his face to make sure he was alert, Detective Inspector Jamie Bridge, woken from sleep in his Lake District hotel room, had studied the pictures on his phone carefully. The brown wash and the sodden clothes which clung to a rounded body were not helpful. It would have been easier to identify a clean body laid out on the mortuary slab. But he understood the imperative of trying to determine as soon as possible whether this was the young woman his force had been looking for, or some other unfortunate. He had taken his time to be sure, keeping Detective Sergeant Hann waiting in suspense, his fingers drumming on the steering wheel reflecting his tension.

"That's not Rita Patel." the DI had said at last. Hann had let out a relieved gasp.

"Even allowing for the effect of the water, the face is the wrong shape and the nose is long and fine where Rita's is, well, more of a blob." he had said inelegantly. His vocabulary at that hour of the night was not extensive. He hoped Rita would never hear exactly what he had said.

"Phew!" Sergeant Hann had said. "Thank you, sir. We'll get on with identifying who this woman is and finding out what happened to her."

"Glad to help." Jamie Bridge had replied, "And I am glad it isn't Rita" he added, thinking that he could go back to bed now; if the body had been Rita's he doubted he could have slept. They had met several times, and he admired the young woman's courage, even if she did take unnecessary risks sometimes. It would have been tragic if it had all ended like this.

"You will need to feed in the results of the post mortem and any identification when the results come through on the body in the river." DI Foster was saying. DS Hann shook himself into life and nodded. "I doubt there is any connection with Rita Patel but we should keep an open mind." she added. Hann nodded.

"Otherwise, we seem to be running out of leads on Rita Patel." DI Foster looked across the table at the Sergeant as if it were his fault. "Run your thoughts by me." she invited.

DS Hann wasn't sure he had any thoughts, but he turned the pages on his notes and offered a few ideas.

"We could do a reconstruction of her last known whereabouts. See if it jogs anyone's memory." he offered.

"Hmmn." DI Foster was not overly impressed. "I think with two women in saris in trouble, one dead and one missing, we need to tread carefully. We don't want to play up the race angle accidentally, especially with this EU referendum coming along. The top brass are very keen on community cohesion and showing how we all get along." she said, reciting a major strategy point from the most recent senior officers' briefing.

"We could get the family to do an appeal and put it out on social media. Rita might see it, if she has gone of her own accord, or it might prick someone's conscience, someone who knows something but isn't directly involved." Sergeant Hann thought he sounded quite coherent on this point.

"Mmmn. Not a bad idea." The Detective Inspector was begrudging. "Set that in motion, will you? Speak to the communications team." Hann wrote himself another action point.

"What's happening about the disappearance of Lateef and Tanisha Kahn? Is there a connection? Is it a coincidence?" DC Hannah Logan, sitting next to DI Foster, spoke up. She had recently joined the expanding team looking for the missing young woman and had taken on the task of collating all the evidence and maintaining continuity.

"The review team looking at the death of Afzal Kahn are checking on it. They will keep us informed." DI Foster replied.

"Anyone got any other suggestions?" the Detective Inspector looked around the table as if this were an initiative test, not an excuse for her having run out of ideas.

After a pause, DC Hannah Logan ventured "We could go over timings again. Check who might have had the means and opportunity to snatch Rita even if we can't be sure of motive yet. I would start with the older brother and the boyfriend. Both could be one of the men that the Big Issue seller saw. She thought one was black and another was Asian.

Mohal was covering a trial for the paper on the Friday that she disappeared, but he could easily have got the detail he needed for his report from another reporter. He has a silver Golf which might fit the Big Issue seller's description."

"Hmmn" now it was DS Hann's turn to sound sceptical. "I just wonder if Mohal would have gone to Caffe Nero and tracked down the Big Issue seller if he was involved?" he said, referring to the amateur sleuthing of Mohal and Priya which had annoyed him, especially the posting of pictures around the town centre. It made the police look inefficient. "It was a big risk if he did do it."

"Double bluff?" DC Logan ventured.

"Yeh, I see what you mean, but Mohal is a stretch, I think, from what I have seen of the family." The Inspector was not keen. "But checking timelines is a good use of our time and the person I think we could look at first is the boyfriend. The Coop manager said he was jumpy on the day Rita disappeared. What if he knew more than he has let on? I think we need to see if we can get him to trip himself up."

Sunday 1ˢᵗ May 2016 1pm

DS Hann managed two hours of glorious unconsciousness on a sofa in the rest room before he and the Inspector made the short drive to Fosse Park, the out of town shopping centre not far from police HQ, where Sue Foster had established that Jacob Johnson would be working that afternoon. A press conference to highlight the social media appeal had been arranged for 5pm that evening. Fortunately, DS Hann kept a razor and a spare shirt in his locker so he was planning to spruce up his appearance before then.

Jacob wasn't hard to spot. He was standing, as he had described to DI Foster, on a corner near Primark beneath the largest picture of a fish that DS Hann had ever seen. The fish came with an arrow and the name of the fish and chip restaurant which was a few metres around the corner. The fish was bright blue in colour, as were the clothes which Jacob wore to draw attention to this tableau.

"Tell us again where you were on Friday 22 April. The day that Rita was last seen." DI Foster asked him as the three of them stood under the fishy sign.

Jacob sighed, crossed one ankle over the other, and leant on the sign as he spoke.

"I do wish she would turn up. This is killing me.." he said, adding, "If you see what I mean."

Then he recited the events of the day so far as he knew them. How he had gone to work at the Coop after reading a few birthday messages, how he had found it hard to concentrate, hoping that Rita would get in touch, how that excitement had turned to anxiety and then disappointment when she didn't and seemed to have turned off her phone. How he had gone home early.

"What time?" David Hann checked his previous notes while Jacob spoke. "I dunno. Eddie said I could go. It was about 3.30 ish?"

"And your car, where was it on that day?" DI Foster this time.

"Outside my house. I didn't want to be tempted to drink and drive, not on my birthday." Jacob tried a winning grin but, as he remembered it was the police he was speaking to, it froze on his lips.

"Does anyone else have use of the car, or access to the keys?" DS Hann avoided the implicit invitation to congratulate Jacob on his responsible choice.

"Well, I leave the keys in the hall in the house I share. Sometimes one of boys asks to borrow it. But they always bring it back in good shape." Jacob explained.

"And did anyone? Borrow your car that day?" the Sergeant checked. This was a new line of inquiry.

"No. That is to say, not as far as I know." Jacob replied

slowly, trying to visualise the day in question. "That's right!" light was dawning on memories made dull by the ingestion of alcohol on his birthday. "I didn't exactly get home after I left work. Jaz was having a smoke in the garden of the pub on the corner and I joined him for a cheeky drink. We ended up staying there all night, apart from the biryani we got on the way home. So, I couldn't say the car wasn't moved. But it was outside the house the next day. When I was desperate to find out what had happened to Rita."

"Remind us when you last saw her, if you would." the DI asked. She thought she saw Jacob hesitate for a moment, but maybe he had just lost his balance. He shifted his weight and stood straighter beneath the fish.

"Well, that depends." he began uncertainly. The officers waited, uncomprehending, while he looked at them both. Then he continued.

"Well we met – actually went out together- a couple of weeks ago. But we spoke every day. Usually several times. So, the last time.." he paused again. DI Foster raised her eyebrows in query, "Would be when we skyped, that was on Thursday, the day before my birthday. She never said she was planning a surprise. Well, I guess she wouldn't.." Jacob's eyes were looking into the distance, not for the first time DS Hann saw Jacob disappearing into his own world. "What did she say?" the Sergeant brought him back to reality. "I understand you told Rita's brother that she had thought of something to do with the trial?"

"Mmmn?" Jacob seemed lost in his thoughts. "Oh, yeh." He blinked hard as if to dispel whatever was passing through his head and focus on the question." It was something about a coat not being a coat. That maybe it was more like a gown. But she wasn't sure if it was the barristers' gowns that had put the idea in her head. I think she was quite disturbed by the questioning in court. She said the more times you described something the less you could be sure what you had seen and what you were remembering from what you said before."

"And that was it?" DS Hann pressed.

"Yeh." Jacob shrugged and nodded.

"We'll need to talk to you again." was Sue Foster's parting note as she turned away, signalling for the Sergeant to do the same.

Behind them, Jacob made an exaggerated bow, like an obliging page boy.

DI Foster was not interested in complicated issues about memory. She wanted evidence and found herself feeling disappointed as she and Hann walked away. Their investigation seemed to be going backwards. Now they had more potential suspects to check on and no firm leads. "Check with his housemates." she told the Sergeant. "Was he telling us the truth about his whereabouts? Could he have left his mates at any time? And find out which of them was where. Could any of them have taken the car and used it to snatch Rita?"

"You don't think we should be looking at the car?" Hann checked.

"We can't justify the resources in checking every white or silver car we come across." DI Foster was clear, reduced budgets and resources being a constant theme at senior officers' meetings. "But check if ANPR picked up either Jacob's or Mohal's car on the day Rita went missing. And tell DC Gardner to let the family know we've spoken to Jacob." Pausing for a moment, she added, thinking how to impress the Chief Constable "We can say at the press conference that we have several lines of inquiry."

Chapter

11

"Nowhere can I think so happily as in a train."

A. A. Milne

Tuesday 3rd May 2016 4pm
11 days missing

It had been a fairytale finish for the champions was the verdict of the Times on the conquering of the Premier League by Leicester City the previous day. As befitted the occasion, the team had celebrated the Chelsea goal against Spurs which gave them the title at Jamie Vardy's house. Meanwhile, Detective Constable Gardner had a nightmare scenario to consider as she composed herself on the doorstep of 10 Elm Drive. There had been a bit of a break through, which her DI had been very relieved to be able to report to the top brass. Now the Constable had to break the news to the family and she wanted to choose her words carefully. The people on the other side of the door knew she had something to tell them. She had tried to sound as neutral as possible when she told Padma that she would be calling round. It was not one of her routine visits, so Padma knew immediately that something out of the ordinary had happened. DC Gardner thought it likely that Rita's mother would have summoned at least one of her sons, if not both, and possibly her sister, Jaina, as well, for moral support. There could be quite a crowd. At least the media had not picked up on anything, yet.

She rang the bell. Padma was prompt to answer and open the door, as if she had been waiting.

"Do come in." she said nervously. DC Gardner followed Padma into what was becoming a familiar kitchen. As she had guessed, Mohal and Nayan were both there. Various national newspapers were strewn across the white kitchen table. The Sun had opted for the headline 'Blue Done It' as they hailed the Foxes' triumph as the greatest footballing story of all time and reported that Hollywood producers were rumoured to be interested in a film on the life of Jamie Vardy. The Guardian, DC Gardner noticed, had opted for 'Leicester City Kings of England' and a picture of Richard III.

"Do sit down." Padma was full of courtesy and good manners.

"You have something to tell us." As she spoke these words, Padma reached for Mohal and Nayan. The three sat together, holding one another's hands, as if to ward off bad news. No one would guess that, only ten minutes before, the two brothers' hands had been locked in a different exercise - a fierce arm-wrestling contest, each accusing the other of cheating while they strained to win the fight. Now they were united in their concern for their sister.

"I do, yes, and I wanted to tell you myself, before the press and social media get hold of it." the Detective Constable paused, aware that Padma was scarcely breathing. The atmosphere in the room was tense.

"It is nothing to do with that unfortunate young woman? The one they found in the river?" Padma's voice was trembling. Nayan and Mohal exchanged looks. According to Twitter, the woman had been identified through a relative's DNA, which the police had on their records. They weren't looking for anyone in connection with the death, which suggested she had killed herself.

"No, no." DC Gardner reassured Padma. "It's something completely different. As I told you, we don't think the body we found had any connection to Rita." she added, then went on "What I have to tell you now is not conclusive of anything. I must emphasise that. It doesn't really take us very much further forward in our inquiries, but.."

"But.." repeated Mohal, "What is it you have found? We need to know." he insisted impatiently.

"Of course. Well, we have found a car. A white car. It was abandoned." she told the three expectant faces.

"The one Rita was taken in? You think that's the car?" Nayan jumped in excitedly.

"We believe it might be, yes. But the reason is – and I don't want you to worry too much about this." DC Gardner swallowed and spoke slowly, but, as soon as she had said these words, she could sense she had just ratcheted up the tension in the room. Best to get it over with she thought. Everyone said this family liaison role was tricky. She had volunteered for it partly because she knew Rita and her family, indeed she had every reason to be grateful to Rita, who had saved her from a fire in the past. But she had also put herself forward as a step towards promotion, which she was sure she merited but which she struggled to convince her bosses she was ready to apply for.

"There was some blood on the car. On a rear door and on the passenger seat at the back. Not a lot of blood, I have to tell you, but we tested it, and it is a match for Rita's, your daughter's." she got the news out quickly.

"No!" Padma breathed out heavily now, like the air being let out of a tyre.

"How much is not a lot?" Mohal, the journalist asked, while Nayan, his imagination going wild, exclaimed, "They cut her? Why?"

"I will tell you as much as we know. Everything else is speculation. We can all make up lurid pictures of what may have occurred, but we have to restrain ourselves. The blood may mean a lot, or it may mean very little, an incidental injury perhaps. There is, as I said, very little of it, relatively speaking. Some drops on the door handle and some more on the passenger seat. Enough for a cut to have occurred, perhaps to an arm or a hand, not enough to suggest any life threatening or really serious injury."

"Life threatening" Padma gasped as she repeated the words. She was looking down at the table now, not at the police officer, as if she did not want to hear any more or was trying to process what she had just been told.

"I am sorry to use the expression. What I mean to convey..." DC Gardner tried to get back to the script she had planned in her head. It was very difficult to find words that would strike the balance between not causing undue alarm but not providing unwarranted assurance. Just keep to the facts DI Foster had said when they discussed how to approach this, "is that it does appear that Rita was in the car, her blood is proof of that. Since the car was stolen and Rita had no connection with it, we are proceeding on the basis that the report of some sort of abduction or woman being forced into a car may have been an actual sighting of Rita." she finished.

"The car was stolen? So, it doesn't help identify who may have taken her?" Mohal was quick to pick up on this.

"It doesn't, no. The car was stolen from a car park at East Midlands Airport, which, again, may or may not be significant. It was reported missing on Sunday, nine days after Rita disappeared. We found it in a street behind Leicester railway station."

"Nine days! Why not sooner?" Nayan was aghast.

"The owner was on holiday. He wasn't very happy when he came back from Corfu to find his car had gone."

"So, the car's a dead end?" Mohal wanted to know. "There's no DNA or fingerprints from anyone else?"

"All I can tell you" this phrase too had been rehearsed. Sometimes it was not a good idea to share everything with the family, however much you wanted to, the DI had said. "is that we have found some evidence of other people in the car, but it hasn't helped us to identify anyone."

"Why?" Padma was dismayed, "Why can't you identify

who has taken my daughter?"

"It means they aren't on the system, mum." Mohal patted his mother's hand reassuringly while looking at DC Gardner for confirmation.

"Yes, that's right. We have some prints and DNA but they don't match anyone who has been in contact with the police sufficiently to leave us their fingerprints or a DNA sample." DC Gardner acknowledged that Mohal was correct in his assumption.

"So, they are amateurs!" Nayan scoffed, "Not even real criminals!" he sounded disgusted, almost disappointed.

"Well it may be a good thing if whoever has taken her is not on their records." Padma found a straw to clutch, "Maybe they are not criminals as such. Perhaps it's a student joke or a silly trick."

"Maybe" Mohal sounded doubtful. He did not want to depress his mother, but neither did he want her to harbour unrealistic hopes. It would be difficult enough if the end result of all this worry was really bad news. "All we know is that they haven't been in trouble with the police before."

"Now they will be" Nayan said defiantly, "When you catch them, I mean" he looked hard at DC Gardner.

"Of course." she said, "When we find out who is responsible then we will consider what they can be charged with." She tried to sound as neutral as possible.

"So, you are working on the theory that she was taken?" Mohal was checking now. "Yes" the Detective Constable confirmed.

"But you don't know by whom, or why, or where they took her?" Mohal tried to keep some of his exasperation out of his voice.

"That's correct, yes" DC Gardner nodded. "There are no sightings after the evidence of the Big Issue Seller, and there is no sign of her on CCTV. We are of course trying to see if we can spot the car on any recordings and we are appealing for dashcam footage that might help us work out what route the car took."

Again, Mohal and Nayan exchanged looks. They had seen the on-line discussions about the reduction in the coverage of CCTV in the city. Budget cuts had eaten considerably into the use of CCTV. The chances of their sister being found by that means had reduced accordingly.

"So where could she be?" Padma started to wail. "And what if she is hurt? What if she needs medical attention? Who will look after her?" and tears started to flow down her face and to fall silently among the good news sprawled in newsprint on the white kitchen table.

Chapter

12

"I was born in Faridabad but brought up in Delhi and Mumbai. My father had been living hand-to-mouth and literally slept on railway platforms when he came to Mumbai for the first time to become a film singer. My parents were both singers; they sang together and fell in love due to their singing."

Sonu Nigam

Missing

Her heart was fluttering as she woke to find herself struggling like a trapped bird. She writhed but couldn't move her arms. She kicked out but couldn't move her legs. What was happening to her? It was too dark to see where she was, to make any assessment. Her efforts were ineffectual and she could feel acid rising from her stomach to her throat. When she stopped trying to wriggle and her heart settled into a better rhythm, Rita started to recognise that something else was paralysing her, apart from the physical restraints; it was fear.

Why was this happening? What was going on? What could she possibly have done to deserve this? Rita fought the pressure of sleep trying to overwhelm her again. She struggled with her mind, trying to wrestle with these questions before the next wave of darkness, which she could sense was readying itself to wash over her, arrived. Who were these people? What could their motive be? And what were their intentions?

Later

Blue. As Rita started to swim to consciousness again, behind her closed eyes all she could see was a city covered in blue: and there was a kindly voice, speaking in an Italian accent, saying liltingly "Justa keep on dreaming." Perhaps she was dreaming? At first what happened had been like an action movie. Now everything seemed blurred and out of focus, as if she was looking at scenes filmed in soft focus.

Later still

When she came round again and opened her eyes, the impression she had of a blue colour was replaced with darkness. The more she peered the less she could see, at first, and she started to panic. Had she gone blind? Gradually, she was reassured to find, the darkness became grey rather than black and unfamiliar shapes started to form themselves. She was alone, which was both a relief and a worry. What if no one came for her? What if someone did come for her? She could feel fear rising through her body again, from her feet through her stomach and heart to her head and with the rush of adrenalin Rita began to twist again, trying to unbind her hands and feet. This did not last long. A numbing tiredness swept down over her like an avalanche and her movements ceased.

Much later

Where am I? How long have I been asleep? Why can't I move? I need to get out of here! It was no use struggling, Rita remembered; she had gone through the same process the previous times she had woken to find herself alone in this strange room, and found she was sitting, bound, on this plastic chair. It was the uniform kind of chair found in communal halls and meeting rooms everywhere. The sort of chair which was okay for an hour or so, but after that your body started to protest at the touch of the chair in various places and you wanted to escape it. As Rita had discovered, she did not have that option. Her legs were bound to the chair with tape, the sort they called gaffer tape she thought, but she had no idea how she knew that or what the name meant. She had been through this irrelevant train of thought before too.

This is like that film Groundhog Day, she said to herself, growling in frustration at herself. I have to find a way of not repeating the same thoughts and actions she resolved. She recalled that she had been afraid that her struggles might tip the chair over, but then she had gathered that the chair was somehow fastened down; it was stuck to the spot, like herself. She would seek to shout for help, only to remember her mouth was silenced by a scarf. An eye mask had been placed round her neck, which she had been told to put on when one of them came to visit her and which she had been told she could remove only when her captor had left the room.

How long had she been here? She wasn't sure. A day or so, perhaps? She could remember two visits, at each of which she had been left something to eat. Already there was a routine, which she was schooling herself to follow, anxious not to antagonise her captors while she tried to work out what was going on.

The eye mask they had given her looked like one of those sleeping masks you get on a plane. No expense spared then. When she had put on the mask as directed the ritual could begin. The man- presumably it was a man, she guessed this from the deep voice and the person's height- would enter the room. Rita had managed to see from under the mask that he wore large brown boots and had what seemed to be a cushion cover over his head, with holes cut for his eyes. When Rita first saw this, she thought it was a joke; then she realised no one was laughing.

He, whoever 'he' was, would bring her food and water, untie her and leave her for about twenty minutes while she ate. During this time, she had been allowed to remove the mask from her eyes and the scarf from her mouth and move around the room while her guard waited outside; she had heard him pacing up and down with heavy nervous steps, ensuring his presence and proximity prohibited her from calling for help. Then he returned to tie her back into the chair.

She had not been idle during these brief breaks. Although feeling groggy, she knew this was her only chance to get some information, so she forced herself to move around as she ate. She had ascertained that the room was small and narrow with a low ceiling and curtains on every wall. The curtains prevented much light from getting in, so she couldn't even tell what time of day it was. The room had a smell of damp. At first, she thought she might be in an attic. But it was cold, and attics were often hot, weren't they?

A bucket had been placed in the corner for her use when they came to feed her. She wasn't sure if the unpleasant smell which attacked her nostrils was coming from the room, the bucket, or herself. She could do with a wash. Her springy brown hair was starting to go limp in the damp atmosphere and bits were sticking to her face. She realised when she shook her head that she was still wearing her gold earrings. How bizarre she must look! Her sari was proving impractical and was part of the reason that she felt cold, as well the fact that her feet were bare, not that the gold sandals would have been much use. Even with her jacket on, the thin material of her clothes was not suitable for her current surroundings, whatever they were. She cursed the fact that she had been so dressed when she was taken. Why wasn't she in her usual shirt and jeans? She had mentioned to her guards (she thought there was more than one, but everything in her head was hazy) that she would like different clothes, but she wasn't sure they had heard or cared. Presumably they had taken her pink satchel bag since it was nowhere to be seen; that meant no iPad and no phone, not that the phone was a great deal of use as she remembered she had run out of credit not long before she was taken. Rita tried not to think about that, and, instead, was starting to long for perfume and gel hand wash when she fell asleep again.

Still missing

Where am I? How long have I been here? Why can't I move! As she woke again, Rita lectured herself; she must put some sensible thoughts together. The trouble was that she was probably being drugged, she realised, which was why she was so drowsy. She was pretty sure any substances were in the bottles of water they gave her to drink, since they seemed to be keeping her on a diet of supermarket sandwiches, which were wrapped when they arrived. At least they were choosing vegetarian ones- so far, she had been treated to three- cheese, salad, and hummus. If she couldn't keep track of the time, she would calculate her captivity in sandwiches, she resolved.

She needed to focus her thoughts, Rita told herself severely, to try to stay awake and to stop herself falling into a well of worry or self-pity. When she let the anger and frustration that she felt die down, this was where her thoughts sank next. She would conjure up pictures of her family- her mother and her brothers, not to mention her aunt, uncle and cousins. Then she would think of her friends- Priya would be so worried as would Sammi and all her uni housemates, as well as friends on the history course and, of course, her boyfriend, Jacob.

How fearful they must be. She wished she knew what they were doing now, but realistically what could they do to find her and get her out of here? If she did not know where she was, or why she had been taken there, how would anyone else work it out? After the self-pity came the anxiety. How dangerous were her captors? What was their motive? Did they mean to hurt her? Would she ever see her home again?

Rita tried to recall how this had happened. Perhaps that would give her a clue. She had been so excited, getting ready in her bedroom at the back of the house in Elm Drive. Before donning her sari – a new one in the blue colour which Leicester City wore, a very popular choice according to the lady in the shop - she had made careful preparations. You needed both hands to dress yourself, and there was no scope for reaching out for anything you had forgotten. If it went wrong, she would have to start again. Wearing a floor length underskirt tied tightly at the waist, and a blouse fitting just below her bust, she had pulled on the sari material and tucked it into the waist of her skirt. Watching herself in the mirror and remembering all that Padma and her grandmother had taught her, Rita had gathered the other end and folded it into six or seven pleats of even width, bringing the end round her waist and dropping the remaining material with a satisfying 'swish' so that it fell at knee level. The pleats she was pleased to see were straight and even. Now she had one arm covered by the material and the other free, while the rest of the dress ran to the floor neatly.

Although she said so herself, she was a vision. Rita had already decorated her hands and face, applying her make up carefully, and pinned up her hair, showing off exotic gold earrings which dangled like decorations from each lobe. She scarcely recognized the smart young Asian woman in the mirror.

Satisfied with her appearance at last, she had snatched up her black jacket and pink satchel bag in order to catch the bus into the city centre, after a brief farewell to her younger brother who was absorbed in something on his telephone screen. Arriving in town, she had called in at Caffe Nero on Granby Street where she worked in the holidays. She had promised to show her friends there her outfit for the evening. Everyone had admired her sari and said how different she looked. "You rock!" Gino had said. How long ago that seemed, a world away.

Her recollections were confused as to how many men had seized her, or exactly how It happened when she stepped out of the café and started to walk to the bus stop. There were three of them, she thought, narrowing her eyes as she tried to remember the encounter in the street. She had not been paying attention; she was walking on the pavement and, like so many people do, talking on her phone. She had been answering a call from Dr Sharma. It was the first time they had spoken since the sudden and terrible death of his wife. Rita had been pleased that he had found the time to ring and wanted to speak to her, but she had found it hard to find the right words. That was why she was concentrating on the conversation and had not noticed the threat around her, she supposed, not that it was normal to walk along fearful of being snatched against your will.

"I wanted to think you for your kindness" Dr Sharma had said, referring to the card and the flowers which Rita had sent, together with two picture books for his young children. "It was very thoughtful of you. Aashi and Sadhil love the books."

"How was the funeral?" Rita had tried to keep the conversation factual as she could hear a crack in Dr Sharma's voice when he mentioned the children.

"It went well thank you. Just a small group. Some friends from Derby, where we lived before, kindly came and Sunetra was there to represent the dental surgery. My wife had no family members in the country and her family in India could not get visas in time, but they were with us in spirit. Everyone here has been very helpful. As advised, we were subsequently able to scatter her ashes in the river Soar, at a leafy spot by the Space Centre. It was very moving. However shocking her death, her spirit is peaceful now, I am sure of it."

"Yes, she is" Rita had agreed. "Thank you for calling me. I know my mother wants you to take as much time as you need before you think of coming back to work."

"Yes, I am sure she is right." Dr Sharma had sighed, "But I feel the need for routine, to be useful." he added. "I will see how it goes."

Then he had said goodbye and Rita had been putting her phone back in her satchel bag, mentally reminding herself to top it up as soon as she could, when two men, who had been approaching her along the pavement, suddenly picked her up off her feet, taking one arm each, and, before she could understand what was happening, had forced her into a car which, she belatedly realised, had been waiting by the kerb.

Chapter

13

"Justice is like a train which is always late."
Yevgeny Yevtushenko

Still missing

If she closed her eyes, she could see the blood again. Perhaps it was because her arm had started throbbing. She could ask her kidnappers for painkillers, but was that a good idea if they were already giving her something to make her sleep? She recalled that she had caught part of her arm on the car because it was exposed by the sari; she had been carrying her jacket on her other arm. It happened as they were wrestling her inside the vehicle. She hadn't felt any pain at the time; when the blood splashed onto the seat Rita had noticed it with a strange detachment, too preoccupied with her predicament to think about it.

When they had lifted her up from the pavement, she had little time to appreciate what was going on, she didn't even panic at the beginning, it was so unexpected. When fear finally arrived and she had started to struggle, the men were too strong. She had got one arm free and tried to wave to attract someone's attention. That was when her arm got caught on the door of the car she thought. She could picture the scene now as if it happened to someone else. The two men were making her get in the car, one pulling and one pushing. Rita found herself sitting inside the vehicle, gasping for breath and trying to wriggle from their grasp, as they pushed her into the middle of the back seat and shut the door. Then the car had set off quickly, with her wedged between the assailants. She had just taken a deep breath in order to protest loudly when a pad was placed over her mouth and nose. It smelt strange and she felt woozy immediately, her head dropping as she fell unconscious.

In her drugged and dreamy state, Rita was finding it difficult to divide reality from her imagination. She squeezed her eyes hard closed to try to picture the men. What had they looked like? The ones on the pavement had been young, she thought. They were certainly strong. They had baseball caps pulled down over their hair and sheltering their eyes from her gaze. One might have been Asian, perhaps and the driver, she recalled, had black dreadlocks emerging from under his cap. They were all wearing dark colours, she thought; their clothes gave no clues as to who they were, or want they wanted.

Did her captors speak? When they picked her up, literally? She thought she could recall one of them swear about her cut arm in the car before she fell asleep "Sh*te! Do something!" There had been panic in their voices as they shouted to one another. The events were disjointed in her mind. Maybe one of them did say something to her at some point, but she couldn't be sure "Don't worry Rita. You will be all right" or had she made that up? Was this personal then? It couldn't be for money – her family weren't rich and, after all, they had not even taken her jewellery from her. Did she hear them say, as she was waking up after the first application of the sweet- smelling substance on her face which had sent her into nothingness, "This should only be for a few days."?

Did she hear that? Memory was a strange thing. It was hard to know what she had heard and what was in her dreams. Was she remembering something real, or something from Netflix - one of Jacob's drama box sets he was so fond of? If only she had someone to talk to, to check her ideas and thoughts. She remembered now; she had been trying to talk to Morwenna about something. What was it she wanted to discuss?

Rita tried to take solace from the fact that her kidnappers were checking on her and were feeding her. They had even taken care of the cut on her arm. When she had woken the first time in the room it was to find a large sticking plaster and bandage expertly applied. On each visit, her guard undid the bandage and changed the plaster, treating her arm with skill and concern. None of this care suggested they wanted to hurt her, she tried to reassure herself as sleep returned.

Later

Waking again, Rita wondered when her captor would return? She didn't know whether to look forward to his visits or dread them in case the routine changed, in case something worse happened. She had read from the testimony of hostages who survived ordeals that it was a good idea to get into a routine, and to exercise. Well that was difficult while she was stuck on this chair with no way of knowing how time was passing.

At least she wouldn't get fat, not on this diet. There was no chance of her turning into a figure like Daniel Lambert. Last May, almost a year ago, on a visit home to Leicester from Warwick University, just before her first-year exams, Rita had seen his picture and some of his clothes and possessions in one of her favourite museums, the Newarke Houses Museum. The museum was made up of two Tudor Houses, one of which was Wigston's Chantry House, named after William Wigston, a wealthy Leicester wool merchant. The chantry, she knew, was established so that masses could be sung for him after his death and so, it was believed by Christians in medieval times, speed his soul on its journey through what they thought of as purgatory, a sort of vestibule to heaven. She found it a strange idea.

Now, to distract herself, she tried to recall what she had learnt about the famous local character Daniel Lambert. Living in Georgian Leicester and weighing 53 stones, he was the heaviest man in recorded history; and people thought there was an obesity problem today! Just like now – Rita thought of programmes like Embarrassing Bodies – people had been fascinated by someone who looked so different. It was the same with Joseph Merrick, she thought, the so-called 'Elephant Man', also born in Leicester, who was exhibited as a freak show in Victorian times because of his deformities.

People paid to see the unusual, and Daniel Lambert when he died in 1809, aged only 39, was on a publicity tour in the nearby town of Stamford. It had taken twenty men to move his coffin, which was on wheels, to the burial ground at St Martin's church there. In the portrait of him that she had seen hanging in Newarke Houses Museum, Daniel was shown in a red hunting coat, she remembered, conjuring up the picture in her mind. She had discovered that he had belonged to a family of gamekeepers and huntsmen and was himself a keen sportsman, although his job was as a jailer, with a reputation for being kind towards the inmates. He had somehow piled on the weight by his mid-twenties. Being so obese must have been like being imprisoned, Rita thought. He would not have been able to go out without considerable help.

Now she could visualize another portrait of Daniel Lambert which she had seen at Compton Verney, the art gallery not far from Warwick where she was at uni. He had a good head of brown hair and sharp brown eyes which looked at you piercingly from within a swollen face of surprisingly healthy-looking, ruddy, flesh. His chin sank into a white collar and he had no neck to speak of. His calf had measured three feet one inch, she had read at the museum, and his waist was nine feet four inches. Definitely not a good BMI! In the Compton Verney picture, two small white hands emerged from the darkness of his jacket which edged around the main feature of the picture, a mustard waistcoat the size of which could only be guessed at. The jacket was clearly not designed to be fastened, and the trail of waistcoat buttons looked under some strain as it curved over the enormous swell of his stomach. The waistcoat bordered on thighs as big as tree trunks encased in black breeches. These were worn above white socks which were squeezed over bulging ankles and descended into black shoes melting into the darkness of the floor. At first, the undulations of his body made you think he was standing, but, on closer consideration, it was apparent that the position of the hands resulted from him having his elbows resting on a chair, and a chair back could just about be seen behind him. Pity the furniture that bore that weight, Rita had thought.

Now she was the one stuck on a chair. Was that why her thoughts had turned to Daniel Lambert? No, it was something else. Try to think, she told herself. The exhibition about Daniel Lambert was in the Newarke Houses Museum. She and Priya had talked about the museum that day last May when they had tried on clothes together. She had been encouraging Priya to sign the petition to save the museum site from sale to De Montfort University. It was when she herself had signed the on- line petition that she had seen the advert for the steam train. That was how she came to book the trip on the Great Central Line in July, which was when she found the body on the train or, to be more accurate, it found her. Why this train of thought? Rita almost smiled at the pun. Was what was happening to her now connected with those events? Somewhere in the depths of her mind Rita became aware that such a thought was stirring, like a heavy anchor being slowly lifted from the sea bed.

Chapter

14

"Mickey Mouse popped out of my mind onto a drawing pad 20 years ago on a train ride from Manhattan to Hollywood at a time when business fortunes of my brother Roy and myself were at lowest ebb and disaster seemed right around the corner."

Walt Disney

Still missing

As she started to wake again, behind her still-closed eyes Rita could see bright lights swaying in the darkness, people swooping and diving to music, lights thrown into the air and caught, costumes shimmering in pools of electric light. She could hear children laughing and calling out excitedly, could hear adults gasping with surprise and pointing out figures to each other. Where was she? Was it the Diwali parade? The annual switch-on in Leicester had taken place on 1 November the previous year, just before she gave evidence in the trial. There had been the usual dazzling display of lights and flames seen by a huge crowd. Why was her mind taking her there? Was she remembering how they had gathered as a group on Belgrave Road to watch the Diwali parade ? Jacob had cried off at the last minute to prepare for a casting and she had been sandwiched between her brothers, with their mother alongside, all linking arms to keep together in the crowd. But Rita didn't think that was the event she was trying to recall. It was another parade in the darkness. What was she thinking of and why?

Waking up a little more, the blackness of the room started to recede as Rita opened her eyes. "Dilly ding, dilly dong." an Italian voice was echoing in her head, telling her to keep awake. It was disorientating to keep dropping off to sleep and not to know for how long, not to know what time of day of day it was, or for how many days she had been kept in this place. Her idea of counting the deliveries of sandwiches was not working very well, the visits were merging in her mind, blurred as it was by whatever substances they were giving her. Perhaps about a dozen sandwiches had gone by, which might mean six days or so? Oh dear, it was better not to count, not to know, it only made her realise how much of her life she was missing out on – the uni work she should be doing, the people she loved that she wanted to see again. Would she ever get back to that life? She vowed if she did that, she would welcome any amount of routine, and she would never again complain about the annoying behavior of her brothers, like their compulsion to arm wrestle each other on any occasion, with arguments about who was cheating and whose wrist was bent.

What had she been thinking of when she fell asleep? A parade? In the dark? Yes, of course, the electrical parade at Disneyland Paris, where she and Priya had escaped to after the trial. Glad to leave behind the burden of their studies for a short time, they had joined in the fun, behaving like their much younger selves as they ran from ride to ride, and watched giant versions of cartoon characters dancing with each other.

Sharing popcorn when the electrical parade passed by in the dark, they had recited the characters' names to one another and waved like everyone else. Was it the train that led the parade that was prodding her mind into a memory, or the light- encrusted dragon which belched smoke from its nose as it travelled along?

As with Belgrave Road during Diwali, Main Street in Disneyland Paris was strung with lights and glowing decorations. There were other comparisons too. All around both parades, conversations were conducted in a variety of languages, many people switching from one to another with great ease. Also, hats were prominent. In Leicester, being at the start of November, the temperature was dropping in the evening when the celebrations began, so people had covered up. In Disneyland Paris, the weather was quite warm for mid- November, but the wind which blew the length of Main Street made it desirable to protect wear headgear. Many in the crowd had opted for Goofy-style hats with large flaps over their ears.

Rita could recall the sound of relentless piped music and parade songs as the giant snails and other creatures span around and brightly-lit frogs appeared with their mouths agape and long tongues protruding. There had been a large bright mushroom, she remembered, bearing an Alice figure. Rita felt a little like Alice now, asked to eat and drink substances and kept in an alternative reality which defied explanation. Alice had been accompanied by a many-legged caterpillar, and butterflies which entranced the younger children in the crowd. Cinderella's coach came next, with her fairy godmother casting her spells and princes and princesses dancing in costumes adorned with light bulbs. Then she recalled the Peter Pan pirate ship and Peter being chased interminably round it by Captain Hook. The actors were full of energy. Jacob had told her it was good temporary work, although he had heard that the staff (or cast members as they were called) were often unhappy with their working conditions and many did not stay for long.

There was a reason why the train-or perhaps the dragon's smoke, or both-stuck in her mind, of course, Rita was starting to realise. She couldn't clear her brain of what had happened last summer. The train! When she closed her eyes, she could see it clearly. It was July last year that she had travelled happily on the heritage railway from Leicester to Loughborough, with her mother and brother, on the treat she had arranged for them. They had found the old train surprisingly comfortable, given its age, as they studied the countryside from the window of the carriage they had to themselves, it being early in the day. The weather was clear, but not particularly warm for the time of year, and they enjoyed the novelty of the smoke flowing past the glass of the windows, dirty with smut already. The smoke was so acrid you could almost taste it. The engine was still spewing out steam proudly as it led the carriages into Loughborough station. It must look like a duck with a flotilla of ducklings floating downstream, Rita had thought. She remembered the engine had hooted, which had stirred excitement among a group of primary school children waiting on the platform. From the train Rita had watched them yelling and jumping on the spot in their pairs, to the consternation of their teachers who were keeping anxious eyes on the platform edge. Then the train was alongside, and the few passengers on board could almost feel the effort of the metal bars attached to the wheels as they moved slower and slower and the engine started to sound like an out of breath athlete, snatching and snorting above the scream of the brakes, then sighing as more steam emerged and the hooter sounded again as the train drew to a halt.

They were quickly ready to step down onto the platform. Rita had gone ahead, turning left towards the rear of the train, to check the timetable for their return journey, leaving Nayan to support the picnic bag and their mother. That was when she had seen a figure at the window of one of the other carriages. Rita seemed to be the only person who had seen it. Most of the travellers, including Nayan and her mother, had turned the other way along the platform, to go to the front of the train and look at the sighing engine and, as she looked around for help, they were lost to view in another cloud of steam.

Instinctively, Rita had run to the carriage where the figure was standing, thinking he or she was having trouble with the door. It was quite a large figure, a bit stooped she thought as she got nearer. She had clasped the handle and pulled on it hard, the door gave way, and the figure tumbled out. Everything went dark for a second, but, before that, Rita thought she saw a figure in black getting out of the carriage on the other side.

By the time she had been questioned by the police and checked out by the paramedics at the station, she, Nayan and her mother had decided not to picnic after all.

"Sorry it spoilt your day" Rita had apologised to her mother as they shared their sandwiches, carrot sticks and fruit on the train back to Leicester.

"Not to worry" Padma had been reassuring. "At least you are all right. And we did get to ride on the train. It's lovely!"

"And it's not every day you see a dead body!" Nayan had put in less than helpfully.

Now she thought back to it, Rita was troubled. What else was there about that day? Something she ought to remember? It was just out of the corner of her mind. There was no definite imprint, just a momentary impression; the thought was like the shadow of a bird flying overhead. Now she was awake for longer – maybe the effect of the drugs was wearing off- Rita felt she should try to recall as much as possible about the train incident in the summer last year, and its aftermath. It might help explain what was going now.

Later

In late July, Rita recalled, a few days after the train trip, she had returned to her routine of shifts at a branch of Caffe Nero in the town centre. She had progressed from the maroon T-shirt of the trainee to the dark blue one of the trained barista, and was versed in all aspects of hot drinks preparation, health and safety and customer relations. She wanted to do as many shifts as she could over the summer, needing to pay towards the rent for her uni house in Leamington, and for the History Department study trip to Venice the next year. Since the cafe boasted the best espresso this side of Milan, it seemed the obvious place. Several of the baristas were Italian, so she got free language lessons at the same time as serving up cappuccinos and lattes. Some of her co-workers provided tutoring and used the café to talk to potential students. It helped to pay the rent for the rooms they occupied in shared houses, which was all anyone could afford these days they told her, the cost of renting having gone through the roof in recent years.

Leaning on the counter at the Caffe Nero, it was Rita's habit to observe the customers as she scanned tables to decide which might need clearing next. The colour scheme of the café was a restful blue and there were books piled on shelves in one corner to give the effect of a place to relax. Many of the books were in Italian, Rita had noticed. Perhaps she should get back to the phrase book in her next break.

She had got used to the rhythm of the place, which varied according to the hours she worked. On an early shift, the office workers would arrive as soon as the pastries were out, seeking their coffee fix to start their day, plus a few construction workers in high-vis jackets and large boots collecting armfuls of lattes and croissants to fuel them for bouts of intense physical activity. After a brief respite, the shoppers and the buggy brigade would arrive, leading to clashes of wheels when shopping trolley met pushchair. The noise levels went up between then and lunchtime. The shoppers were mainly female and used the cafe for a rendezvous and a chat; the young mums tended to get their buggies into a circle and form a sort of camp, looking at their phones and exchanging news on nappy rash and nurseries, pausing to lift out a bawling infant or placate a whining one. Just as they left, the lunchtime rush would start, some busy office workers frantically buying the first sandwich they could find, others luxuriating in time to make decisions slowly and creating a longer queue as they pondered over which flavour of latte to have.

Lunch was quickly followed by the arrival of schoolchildren; they seemed to leave lessons earlier and earlier these days. They would lounge on the soft benches with their legs stretched out and their feet a tripping hazard for other customers. Some got out homework and tried to study, but most would spend the time exchanging gossip and looking at their phones, often ordering one drink and a toasted sandwich between them. Finally, the evening couples arrived, some using the café to meet before going on elsewhere.

One particular late shift stayed in her mind. There had been an amorous couple on the sofa who didn't look like they were going anywhere soon, they were so engrossed in looking into each other's eyes. They contrasted with the sad couple sitting awkwardly at the big table. She had a tissue clutched in her hand which she dabbed at her cheeks from time to time, he kept looking round as if hoping for rescue- this looked like a break-up conversation Rita thought. It would have been insensitive to clear the tables near the couples, Rita had thought, so Rita she had continued to wipe down the counter and tidy the remaining pastries and muffins.

That was when Jacob and his friends had wandered in, looking in need of hydration.

Jacob caught Rita's eye immediately. "Hey, don't I recognise you?" was his opening line.

"I don't think.." Rita began automatically. This happened quite a lot. Then she looked again at the man in front of her.

He was black with an athletic build. He reminded her of that Jamaican runner, Yohan Blake. He was a good bit taller than she was. His eyes were intense as he gazed down at her and she realized that, yes, they had met before.

"Oh yes" she conceded, as she began to make his Frappuccino. She had her back to him, so she had to turn to continue speaking, and to shout above the noise of the ice machine. "You're an actor. I saw you in a production of Romeo and Juliet in Abbey Park."

"You are right fair damsel." Jacob replied in a mock theatrical tone. "I think you helped at Sundial? You were around when one of our Company was killed?" Jacob reminded Rita of the summer she had spent, with Priya, working at a guest house owned by their friend, Athena Maitland.

"We were just doing a street performance out there." he pointed in the direction of Granby Street. "To advertise our production of Much Ado About Nothing. Caused a bit of agitation with some locals, but what can you say." he offered her a leaflet, "You should come and see it."

"Is this how you drum up an audience?" Rita had teased as she placed his drink in front of him and stamped his loyalty card with a red mark.

"I have other ways." Jacob had swaggered a little, "What are you doing after your shift for example?"

So, things had begun. Jacob was different from anyone Rita had known before. He wasn't hard working, like her uni friend Sammi, but neither was he as lazy and relaxed as her brother Mohal. He was a puzzle to her. Jacob could be very quiet and unassuming, until he was put on a stage. Then suddenly he transformed into a character, full of life and interest. You never knew what to expect. Early in their relationship they talked about their families. Rita told him that her grandparents had come to Leicester from Uganda, bringing her parents as small children. Jacob said that his parents were born in the city, but his grandparents had come there from Jamaica. It felt like they had something in common.

The first meeting in July led to more over the summer. As well as acting in the play in the park, Jacob had some work as an extra in a tv drama being filmed in the city about Joe Orton, a local playwright. Orton, he told Rita, had lived in the Clarendon Park area as a small child and then moved to a council estate on Saffron Lane. The scenes they were filming related to his parents; apparently, Orton's father was a gardener for the Council and his mother worked in a shoe factory. The film makers were improvising the sites as best they could, using old buildings around Leicester. Jacob pointed out to Rita the bright pink BASE signs which showed the support crew where to go. They had set up in a car park in Aylestone Park. He indicated the green LOC signs too; these showed where filming was taking place.

"It's mostly sitting around waiting." Jacob had told her as they ate vegetarian burgers in the catering van.

Later

A bit like giving evidence in court, Rita now thought as she recalled their date by the van. You waited ages, then you were in the spotlight, and had to be ready to act your part; but it lasted for only a short time and was a small bit of the whole show.

There it was again, teasing her. Something about the incident on the train and the evidence she had given. She had an idea that she had discussed something about all this recently. What was it? And who had she spoken to about it?

Chapter

15

"The only way to catch a train I have discovered is to miss the train before."

G K Chesterton

Still missing

The drugs seemed to be having less effect, she thought. She was more alert when her captor came to feed her. In fact, she had noticed that it did not seem to be the same man every time. She determined to be more observant, and saw, beneath the thin mask, that one of them was taller and broader than the other. If she was going to try to escape, perhaps she should try to do so when the shorter one was there? Would he be easier to fight? What was she thinking? Men were generally stronger than women, as she knew from arm wrestling with her brothers. Nayan had not been very old when he was able to beat her. A violent struggle was not likely to be successful, Rita thought. She needed to use her brains.

Now that she was awake for longer periods, she had time to think, and her thoughts turned to the reason for this ordeal. If she could work out why this was happening, perhaps she could think of a solution. Her predicament must be something to do with the trial, she had decided. That was the only thing that made sense. In which case, it was all the fault of Thomas Cook, Rita thought wryly to herself. A member of the Temperance Society, the first trip he arranged, in July 1841, was by train from Leicester to a teetotal rally in Loughborough. He set off an explosion of interest in group travel, in 1851 arranging for 150,000 people to travel to the Great Exhibition in London and a few years later he began organising excursions abroad. But for him she might not have been drawn to the advert for the Great Central Railway, or thought what a good idea it would be to treat her mother to a trip on the steam train, which ended up with…

The trial. Maybe if she focused on that. It was a horrible experience, far worse than having a body fall on top of you. If she forced herself to relive her evidence, then maybe whatever it was that was pestering her about it would come back to her.

Just before she had gone back to uni in September, her barista skills well- honed in Caffé Nero by then, Rita had started to receive letters from the Crown Prosecution Service. They notified her that she would be called as a prosecution witness in the trial of Tanisha Kahn, the daughter of the deceased, who the police had charged over the summer. At first, she hoped she could get out of it, but Edward Maitland, Morwenna's father, a lawyer, got a colleague who practiced in criminal law to advise her. He told Rita that wasn't an option. You had to cooperate or get into trouble yourself, apparently.

The lawyer had said that it often took several months, or longer, for trials to take place, because of all the people involved.Unluckily for her, the arrangements for this trial seemed to be taking shape quite quickly and ,in November, it seemed the hearing was going ahead. Rita had dutifully travelled to Leicester with a black suit she had bought for the purpose. The following day, having gone through airline style security at the court entrance, she had found herself in a waiting area, cradling a cup of mint tea and wondering how long all this was going to take. Which was pretty much all that happened that day. Fortunately, she had brought some reading material related to her course, but the time still dragged and it was hard to concentrate. It was tantalising to think the trial was going on so close to where she was sitting, but she was not allowed to watch until she had given her evidence. Mohal was inside the courtroom, she knew, covering the case for his paper. They had agreed not to speak about it. She knew he would give her the details afterwards.

The next day started in the same way, except that the new suit was looking slightly crumpled after a day spent sitting around in it. It was about 11.30 when she heard her name being called. She followed the usher to the court room, trying to use her hands to ease out the creases in her skirt as she walked, and patting down her hair, which had decided to spring out of the style she had coiled it into before she left home. The usher took her to the witness box and invited her to enter.

To Rita's left were the jury members, their heads appearing above a wooden rail as if they were a fairground attraction. Rita tried not to catch their eye but to see them as an amorphous crowd. To Rita's right was the defendant, Tanisha Kahn, sitting head to toe in black including her face veil, her features and thoughts impenetrable.

The prosecution barrister, a portly man who put Rita in mind of a Dickens character – Mr. Bumble perhaps, or Mr. Pickwick- took her gently through her statement. There were no surprises and Rita's heart rate started to settle down.

Then the defence barrister stood up, and Rita took the opportunity to have a swallow from the glass of water before her, causing the barrister, a willowy figure with red hair protruding from under her wig, to cough as if Rita was not paying sufficient attention.

"So, Miss Patel, you travelled on the Great Central Railway from Leicester to Loughborough on the morning of 14 July this year."

"Yes, that's right." Despite wanting to sound confident, Rita's voice had cracked at her first reply to the defence lawyer.

"And you have told the court that you came to be there as a treat for your mother?"

"Yes, that's right." Rita could hear her repeating herself

in her anxiety about the sort of impression she would be making on the jury.

"Our father – her husband-" oh dear, she was starting to sound like an idiot – "He, well, he died recently and me and my brothers .." (that wasn't grammatical, was it? Why was she speaking like this?) "Well we try to find things to cheer my mum up and we thought that.."

"Yes, well, we are all sorry to hear about the loss of your father and the need to help your mother" the barrister broke in briskly, as if Rita were wasting her time, although she was only answering the question. Feeling indignant, Rita barely heard the next question,

"…together?"

"I'm sorry. Could you repeat the question?" Rita had to say. (Oh no, this was not going as she had hoped.)

"It's quite simple" the barrister said abruptly as she adjusted the wig on her head in irritation and looked at Rita as if she was being deliberately awkward.

"You were on that part of the platform at Loughborough station alone? Why were you and your family not together? Why did you split up when the train pulled in?" she asked, staring at Rita for an answer.

"Oh" now Rita understood. "Nayan, my brother, wanted to look at the engine. He's a bit of a nerd – enthusiast." At this slip, Rita thought she could hear a snort from the press gallery where her older brother was sitting.

"He went to the end of the platform with my mother to show her the engine." she continued with the explanation.

"But you didn't go?" the barrister made it sound like Rita had been awkward about it.

"I wanted to check the timetable, which was at the other end of the platform. To make sure we caught the right train back. On-line timetables are all very well but…" Rita's voice trailed off as she saw the barrister was looking at her notes as if waiting for Rita to finish.

"Quite." she said in a clipped tone.

"There was a group of school children at the station, looking at the engine – probably from a primary school." Rita stumbled on, trying to paint the scene.

"Yes. Yes. I'm sure we get the picture, Miss Patel" the barrister was anxious to move on.

"I just wanted to help. I saw a man struggling to get off the train. I was the only one who noticed him." Rita finished lamely as the barrister wriggled her black gown on her shoulders and consulted her notes.

"You went up to the carriage and pulled open a door?" was the next question.

"Yes." Rita kept it short this time.

"And as you did so, Mr. Kahn fell out." the barrister stated this flatly, as if bodies fall out of trains every day.

"That's right. Obviously, I didn't know it was Mr. Kahn then." Rita added to be accurate.

"Quite" the barrister said again and gave a false smile. "Now we come to the part I'm interested in.." she said, as if Rita had been deliberately delaying getting to that point.

"Mr. Kahn- who we now know was dead or dying at the time – fell out of the carriage on top of you." the barrister set out the facts.

"Yes. He sent me flying." Rita found she had turned slightly and was addressing herself to the judge now. She, at least, was looking at Rita, through her large spectacles, while the defence barrister kept looking down while Rita spoke. Rita thought to herself now that, if she had been feeling more confident, she could have addressed the jury, like in films, and turned the case there and then. But she hadn't felt confident; she hadn't wanted to give evidence at all. The police and the CPS had insisted; as Edward's colleague had told her they would. They had threatened to compel her to give evidence if she didn't appear. Now she could picture herself standing there awkwardly, waiting for the red-haired barrister's next question.

She wanted it to be over. She had thought that being involved in a murder trial would be exciting. But it certainly wasn't exciting to be a witness. It was nerve-racking.

"Tell us about that fall. You were knocked backwards onto the platform, then what happened?" the barrister spoke again.

"Yes. I found myself lying on the concrete of the platform with this man, who I had gone to help, sprawled on top of me. He was quite heavy. I couldn't understand why he didn't get up." Rita saw she was waving her arms about as if this would help her description of the events. She stopped abruptly and put them by her sides, wanting to appear sure of herself.

"Quite" the barrister said crisply, "And didn't something else happen? Just as the two of you fell to earth as it were?" she turned to the jury to check they got the humour.

"Well." Rita was fairly sure she knew what the barrister wanted her to say. It had been in her witness statement after all.

"Yes?" now the barrister was tapping her nails on the table in front of her, wanting Rita to speak. "My head hit the ground. Quite hard. I had a bruise for a while."

"Your head hit the ground" the barrister said slowly, as if Rita had admitted to some awful crime.

"Thank you, Miss Patel." her inquisitor's tone was sarcastic, almost suggesting that Rita had been withholding this information.

"And did you lose consciousness at all?"

Rita sensed the barrister was not interested in her health. "No, I don't think so." Rita's voice was sounding weirdly weak; she took another sip of water from the glass in front of her.

"Or suffer blurred vision?" Another query about her condition which did not sound genuine.

"Not really" Rita was starting to sound defensive.

"Suffer enough of a blow to the head as to affect your

account of what you say you saw next?" Now her questioner was getting to her point.

"No, I don't think so." Rita realised she sounded unsure.

"So, to be clear Miss Patel," the barrister proceeded to repeat Rita's words, exaggerating the uncertainty as she did so.

"You don't <u>think</u> you blacked out. You didn't <u>really</u> have blurred vision. You don't <u>think</u> the blow to your head affected what you say you saw next?" she paused for effect.

"Yes" Rita said quietly as if she were a small child caught in a lie.

"And is it true, Miss Patel" (Oh dear what was coming next? Rita wondered, wishing this ordeal could be over.)

"Is it true that, not so very long ago, you were attacked? You suffered a blow to the head sufficient to knock you out? Indeed, so severe that the doctors kept you in a coma for a few days while the swelling in your brain went down?" the barrister was talking quite loudly now, as if to impress the facts upon the jury.

"Yes, that's right" said Rita, recalling how, a couple of years or so ago, a baseball bat had connected with her head while she was investigating a mysterious death at the National Space Centre in Leicester.

"But I recovered. I was given a clean bill of health." Rita tried to justify herself.

"That may be so" said the lawyer, as if this was a matter of conjecture, "But who knows what the effect of a second blow to so delicate a part of the body might be? At least a degree of confusion and disorientation might be engendered in a healthy person, let alone one who had previously sustained an almost fatal blow." she observed to the court in general.

"Well" Rita tried to respond.

"Moving on." the barrister made it seem like Rita was prevaricating.

"Miss Patel, you are lying.." the barrister paused again for effect, was she accusing Rita of not telling the truth?

"You're lying on the ground, having opened the door to the carriage and got more than you bargained for. You're lying.." as she repeated the word, Rita had shuffled uncomfortably in the witness box.

"What you tell us you saw, lying dazed and confused on the concrete.." How many times was she going to repeat it? Rita wondered.

"Well I wasn't.." she tried to interrupt.

"You weren't what? Dazed? Confused? With respect Miss Patel, you have only been able to tell us you don't think you were knocked out, you don't think you had blurred vision. A strange man had fallen on you, when you opened the train door, an unusual circumstance to say the least. You found yourself trapped under his lifeless body. Are you telling me you weren't confused?" the barrister fiddled with her gown again as if she found Rita an irritant.

"Well, no, but " Rita tried to explain.

"Good." the barrister continued briskly, "So, as I say, lying confused and probably dazed, at the least, under the weight of Mr. Kahn's dead body, you say you saw.." The barrister had picked up a copy of Rita's witness statement as if by holding it up she could understand it better. She peered at it closely, reducing its credibility for the jury with every second that her nose nearly brushed the pages.

"'Another figure, a person, was in the carriage'" she quoted, "That's what you said?"

"That's right" Rita confirmed.

"A figure, you say here, which was dressed in black and flew away from the other side of the carriage,.." the barrister paused before continuing, "like a bat."

The last three words the barrister addressed to the jury with a smile.

Then she turned back to Rita, "Really Miss Patel, such florid language. Are you sure you weren't concussed and having a dream at that point?"

"No, I'm sure I wasn't" Rita had asserted.

"You didn't really see a figure, did you?" she asked next.

"Yes, I saw someone who disappeared.." Rita replied quickly.

"Who disappeared." the barrister leapt on the phrase, "Yes, that's the problem isn't it? Because even if we assume you were right and there was a figure, no one else saw this person. How do you account for that?"

"Well, it's hard for me to say what others were doing, I was flat on the ground. Mr. Kahn's shoulders were blocking my view." Rita did her best.

"Quite." The barrister took off her reading glasses, as if whatever Rita had to say did not deserve further examination.

"There was a lot of shouting and confusion. The person must have escaped through the door on the other side of the carriage, gone across the line and got out of the station that way, I would think." Rita speculated.

"Mmmn. You would think." the lawyer repeated Rita's words again so that they sounded feeble, "But it is only a matter of conjecture, Miss Patel. Your conjecture. It was all in your mind. No further questions" The barrister had suddenly sat down before Rita, who was led away by a court official, could protest.

Chapter

16

"If God had intended us to fly, he'd never have given us railways."

Michael Flanders

Still missing

She was allowed into the court after her cross examination. Rita had seen some of the other witnesses, and the evidence of the defendant, Tanisha Kahn, but she had left Leicester before the barristers gave their closing speeches to the jury. By the time the verdict came in, Rita was in Disneyland Paris with Priya. At Priya's suggestion they had snatched a long weekend, to enable Rita to recover from the trial, and Priya to rest from too much studying. The young women had also arranged to meet up with their friend, Morwenna Maitland, and her boyfriend, Lucas, in Paris, on their journey back.

They had been strolling arm in arm on Main Street, lost in a world of giant mice and dogs, princesses, beasts and dragons, and eating warm chocolate croissants, when Rita's phone rang. Rita paused to answer it, saying to her friend, "It's Inspector MacAllister, I'd better take it."

"Hello? Rita?" the Inspector's familiar sharp voice sounded in her earpiece. "I said I would call you when we had the verdict."

"Yeh" Rita's throat was dry, dreading what he might be about to say.

"It was not guilty." the Inspector tried not to sound too disappointed.

"But thanks for your evidence. We'll keep the file open. Another team will take a look. See if we missed anything.

Hope you're enjoying your break." The Inspector ended the call.

"Not guilty?" Priya had guessed as she watched Rita thoughtfully put her phone back in her pocket.

"Your evidence didn't help the police, then?" Priya tried to guess at her friend's feelings since her face had a blank, stunned, expression.

"Rita?" Priya ducked to get in her friend's eyeline. Startled, as if her thoughts had been far away, Rita addressed her at last.

"Yeh. I guess" she stuttered, then she started to justify herself, "I had to say what I saw. I never really thought Tanisha had done it myself, but the police seemed pretty sure. Besides…" Rita's voice tailed off. She was looking into the distance again, all the way down Main Street to Sleeping Beauty's castle, and beyond.

"Besides?" Priya echoed. What did she mean? Priya knew Rita was fond of solving murder mysteries. She wasn't going to try to solve this one, was she?

"Oh, I don't know" Rita shrugged, "I just wish I could remember properly what happened."

"One day perhaps they will be able to put you in a scanner and tell for themselves." Priya told her, recalling a lecture on the subject she had attended "At least that's the science fiction version of developments in neuroscience. It's much more likely that they will be able to predict and prevent the onset of memory loss than that they will be able to help people recall events, although no one is sure. It is all at an early stage of research"

"Oh, let's forget about it and enjoy ourselves!" Rita had shaken her head as if to clear it of the idea nagging inside it. "It's the film studios tomorrow, yeh? And where are we meeting Morwenna on Sunday?"

"She said she'd text. A café near the gig she thought." Priya replied, happy her friend seemed to be snapping out of her introspective mood.

"What's the band called again? The one they are seeing?" Rita was glad to talk about something other than the trial.

"Eagles of Death Metal" Priya told her.

"And where are they playing?" Rita had asked.

"It's a night club. It's called The Bataclan." Priya replied.

Still missing

The darkness was absolute when Rita opened her eyes this time. It must be night? Was she alone? Suddenly she was alarmed -was there someone else in the room? Was that why she had woken up? Had she heard something? In the dark your hearing is sharpened, especially when you are afraid for your life. Who had said that? Your ears act as your eyes. You tune into every sound, you listen for each sign of danger. That is what Morwenna had said,as she told Rita about what it was like to cower under a table in a darkened night club while gunmen roamed the premises, intent on dispatching concert attenders in between their cries of "Allahu akbar". She listened closely. There was nobody there was there? Surely, she was alone? Sitting in the black, the darkness enfolding her like a shroud, Rita shivered. Would she ever be found? Would she -she hesitated to think it- would she die here? Would this be her last place on earth, wherever and whatever it was? This is what Morwenna thought, Rita recalled, thinking back to the choking emotion of their conversation when they had been reunited at the Gare du Nord in Paris that November evening.

"I lay so still Rita, hiding under the table, afraid to even breathe. All those hiding games you play as children, it doesn't prepare you for the real thing, for keeping out of sight and out of earshot when your very life depends on it. And all the while hearing the shots and trying not to cry out in alarm, or fear, or pity, for the people who weren't as lucky as you in that moment. And then feeling guilty that it wasn't you who was shot, and relieved at the same time. You listen for every step, every creak of a floor board or squeak of a shoe, the brush of fabric, you feel the air when someone passes near you. This must be what it is like to be pursued in the jungle by a hungry animal, you need all your basic instincts, all your senses have to kick in to protect you. When you don't hear anything for a while, your nerves relax a little, you realise how tense you were holding yourself, you can hear your spine snap into a more comfortable alignment. Then you start to worry. How will I get out of here? How will anyone know I am here? What if they set off a bomb? Has this time of hiding been wasted? Did I switch off my mobile? – I don't want to alert them to my presence. But should I switch my phone on? So that someone can find me, so that I can send another text?"

Morwenna had told Rita that, when it started, they were unsure what was happening. It was hard to comprehend that it was anything bad. Everyone was having a good time, the band were just getting into their set and then, within a minute or less, they realised that things were going horribly wrong, that an evil presence had taken over the venue. Everyone reached for their phones and started making calls or sending messages. That was her last text, HELP GUNMEN AT THE BATACLAN! It was when they realised that they could not get out of the nightclub, that they were being held as hostages or worse, that Lucas had said they should turn off their phones. They lay huddled together, vaguely aware that around them others were doing the same, but too afraid to call out. Is this what it was like in the concentration camps? Morwenna had found herself thinking. Everyone lying together, waiting to see who would be chosen to die next? Is this what it was like in the cattle trucks when the Nazis transported the Jews? Is this what IS were doing to human shields in the middle east today? How can humans treat others like this? She had never known fear like it, Morwenna said, and it was evident from the way she told her story disjointedly. The gunmen spoke little, there was no way to understand them as human beings, any more than they seemed to understand that the people they were killing were human beings too. Occasionally there would be a cry of "God is great!" which sounded more like a battle cry, or a means of bolstering up bravado, rather than a religious statement or a prayer to a divinity. And what divinity would desire such horror, such pitiless destruction? Morwenna had no great faith in God, she told Rita on the Eurostar back to London, but she had enough to feel that God was sad that day, that whatever deity surrounds us was weeping alongside the wounded and the dead, was somehow holding the suffering to himself.

"We just went to enjoy ourselves!" she had wailed every so often as the train sped through the darkness of the Channel Tunnel, "What is wrong with that?" she kept repeating.

"Whatever grievances these people have, it can't be the fault of a band and their fans. Or of people at a football match either." she added, since they were aware by then of the other incidents in Paris that night

'Run.Hide.Tell.' that was the official guidance for terrorist attacks now, Rita knew. Well, what was happening to her wasn't terrorism, as far as she could tell, but she couldn't run and she couldn't hide; all she could do was stay alive so that she could tell her story, like Morwenna had done.

Rita realised her situation was far far different. She knew now that she was alone. There was no lurking gunman, no immediate threat to her life as far as she knew. Nevertheless, she knew fear and uncertainty. Would she ever get back to her normal life? Would she see her brothers and her mother again? What about her exams and all her hopes for the future? What was going to happen to her? While these anxieties circulated around her brain, another idea was forming in her mind again; that she had spoken to Morwenna recently. Was it something about her evidence at the trial? About the 'bat person' who had disappeared? She felt it was important to remember.

Chapter

17

"I never travel without my diary. One should always have something sensational to read in the train."
Oscar Wilde

Still missing

Rita was glad when her captor brought her the change of clothes she had requested. It seemed to her a good sign that he had listened and cared enough to respond. It had been a relief to get out of the sari too, even though the alternative was a set of overlarge grey sweat pants, a black T shirt with a Superdry logo, and a grey jumper, together with socks which were comically big on her feet but long enough to keep her knees warm. The sari now lay in a blue pool on the floor, like the shed skin of a snake. At least this outfit was more practical and she was a bit warmer too. But, if she managed to effect an escape, what would she look like? It was as if she was disguised. Would even her family recognize her?

She recalled from her Civil War studies that there were stories of the future Charles II escaping the clutches of the Parliamentarians in a variety of disguises. It must be her captivity that was making her remember these incidents, she thought. Charles II had been disguised by Catholic sympathisers as a woodsman after he a failed attempt to recapture the throne of his dead father ended when the Royalists lost the battle of Worcester in 1651. He had changed his clothes at a house called 'Whiteladies' and allowed his hair to be cut, the tall figure of the would-be king being hard to disguise. Rita recalled she had read that he put on a green jerkin, grey cloth breeches, a leather doublet and greasy soft hat. His face was stained with walnut juice and the shoes they gave him were too small and hurt his feet. His outfit was no better fitting than hers, she thought. That was the occasion when, while the Parliamentarian soldiers scoured the woods for them, he and Major Carlis had hidden in an oak tree in the Boscobel area for an entire day, only daring to come out and seek sanctuary in a house nearby as night fell.

Travelling westwards after that escapade, Charles II's party went to Bentley Hall where Colonel Lane's daughter was due to visit her sister, who was about to give birth, at Abbots Leigh near Bristol. This time they dressed Charles as a servant but, despite his disguise, his behaviour threatened to give him away. He did not know how to ride a double horse and kept forgetting to doff his cap. After some close calls and betrayals, Charles moved from Lyme Regis and Charmouth to Sussex where he eventually caught a boat called The Surprise from Shoreham. The restoration of the monarchy in 1662 is celebrated by recalling the tree episode, Rita knew, on 29 May, known as Royal Oak day. She wondered what the date was now? Would she be free by Royal Oak day? She fervently hoped so.

* * *

A loud noise woke Rita from her slumber. Like the sound of someone throwing gravel at the walls and the roof of her prison. That couldn't be happening, could it? No, she listened more carefully in the gloom. There it was again – a rumble of thunder. There must be a storm, she thought, and the sound was either heavy rain or even perhaps hail? It had been known even at unlikely times of year. How she longed to know what was happening in the outside world. She missed the feel of fresh air on her face, the sound of traffic, the hum of people and their activities that reminded you that you were alive and part of something. Being held here in isolation, Rita started to wonder if she was losing her identity, losing her mind. How wonderful it would be just to be out there, standing in the rain! She needed to concentrate on thoughts that would keep her company, she decided, memories that would keep her sane until she could get away from here. She would get away, wouldn't she?

Her captor would not talk to her no matter what tactics she tried. It did not stop her from talking to him, though. She had read that it was important to try to bond with your captors, to get them to see you as a human being. She told him about her history studies, and related anecdotes about her brothers which she thought he might find amusing. She tried sympathising with his plight. "Oh dear, this must be tedious for you. I hope it isn't going to go on too long?" Nothing. Well, even if he wouldn't communicate with her, she resolved to ask if he would communicate with the outside world on her behalf. If she could get a message to her family that would be something, wouldn't it?

Chapter

18

"Like all great travellers, I have seen more than I remember, and remember more than I have seen."
Benjamin Disraeli

Still missing

Even with the drugs, Rita's spells of unconsciousness on the chair were getting shorter, but they were filled with dreams from which she would wake, trembling. Perhaps it was a form of delayed shock, she wondered. Clothes came into her dreams a lot – people changing their clothes, especially cloaks and long coats, like the one she could remember Doctor Who wearing, with a long scarf. Was it because of these temporary clothes? Or was her brain trying to remind her of something, the thing to do with the train and the trial; the thing that she thought she could remember until she tried, and then it swam away, like a fish evading the bait.

* * *

Go back to the time before the train incident, her mind told her. Try not to think about it, and maybe your memory will mend itself, perhaps it will patch over the hole that is preventing you from recalling whatever it was, and who she had told. She was pretty sure it wasn't Priya that she had confided in, so thinking about conversations with her should be safe ground. What about that day in May when they were both back from uni for the weekend? When they had gone clothes shopping in the centre of Leicester ? They had called in at Jigsaw and tried on some dresses they couldn't possibly afford, admiring themselves in the mirrors before politely declining. "I didn't like them anyway." Priya said. "Nah" Rita agreed, "Not our style."

As if to make up for the composure they had shown in Jigsaw, they had giggled their way around T K Maxx in the Haymarket shopping centre, finding a row of expensive and impractical-looking cloaks. "Who would wear these?" they puzzled as they took them off the hangers and swathed their bodies in the fabrics. "Someone wanting to hide themselves?" Rita had suggested, "They would make a great disguise."

There it was again, an idea that kept half-formulating itself. Stop trying, Rita admonished herself. Where did we go after TK Maxx? Oh yes, they had walked across the city centre again to the Highcross shopping centre and went into Top Shop.

It was while in the changing rooms there, Rita remembered, that she had told Priya to sign the petition to save the Newarke Houses Museum from sale to De Montfort University. She had told her friend about the cannon ball holes in the walls, made by both sides in the course of losing and retaking the city during the English civil war, and that one of the buildings which formed the museum, Skeffington House, had been occupied by a Parliamentarian family in that period.

Priya had been trying on tops for her spell on the ward as part of her pre-clinical training at Oxford. "I need something professional looking but not too smart and off-putting." she told Rita, explaining that the men who were training had quickly adapted to the male doctor look - brown chinos and a pale shirt - while for the women it was harder to find the right combination "You end up wearing black if you're not careful" Priya had said, "and that is not good for anyone's morale."

Rita could picture her friend now, examining herself in the mirror, testing out a maroon top and then a green one and flicking her black brown hair over the necklines. How she longed to see Priya again!

"The Civil War ended badly for the King, didn't it?" Priya had queried, indulging her friend as Rita gratefully recognised "Seventeenth century? Cavaliers and Roundheads and all that?"

"Yep." Rita had confirmed in a strained voice as she tried to put on a pair of jeans. Somehow the ones in Top Shop never seemed to fit her properly.

"Leicester came off badly too, but Oxford survived pretty well."

"How come?" Priya's voice was muffled as her head was encased in the maroon top which she was removing.

"Well, when Charles I lost the first battle of the war - at Edgehill - he couldn't get back to London, and set up his capital in Oxford instead. It remained a Royalist stronghold throughout the war. The Colleges supported him, and even melted down their plate to make coins; the ordinary people were less keen, especially as they had to share their scarce food with the soldiers. The King lived at Christ Church, the Queen at your college, Merton."

"What about Leicester?" Priya wanted to know.

"Our city was held by the Parliamentarians" Rita told her."Both cities came under siege eventually. Their fates were linked." she went on.

"How come?" Priya prompted.

"To attack Oxford, where the King was, the Roundhead troops had to cross the river, which was tricky. They tried a few times and made it as far as Headington. The King watched them from the top of Magdalen tower. Eventually, towards the end of the war, Fairfax succeeded in entering Oxford with his troops and Oxford agreed a negotiated a surrender. Meanwhile, in order to draw the Parliamentary troops out of Oxford, so the King could get away, Prince Rupert attacked Leicester, making the first of the cannon ball holes in the Newarke. The Royalists were ruthless in their attack and in their treatment of the townspeople. Sure enough, Fairfax left Oxford to go to try to retake Leicester. The two sides met at Naseby. The Royalists were outnumbered and lost. They scattered. Lord Loughborough had been left by the King to defend Leicester, but he did a pretty poor job. When the Roundheads attacked, making cannon ball holes in the Newarke in the same place as the Royalists had 18 days previously, he surrendered, seeing it was a thankless task, and there was no point in losing more men. Once again Leicester was taken, but at a cost to the townspeople, who suffered greatly once more. The relief of Leicester was celebrated in Parliament and they raised some money to help the citizens. There is a day -19 June - called The Relief of Leicester Day. Oxford came out of the war pretty well intact. All the Parliamentary side did when they got it back was to take down some defensive walls. But Leicester suffered badly. The war made it economically weak and it took years to recover." Rita shook her head.

"And the King was executed?" Priya had asked as they waited to pay for their items. "Yes." Rita confirmed. "He was very brave and wore two shirts, as well as his cloak, to make sure he did not shiver and look afraid."

Another jolt of her memory, almost like an electric shock, woke Rita from her reminiscences. What was it her brain was trying to tell her? Something about cloaks? There it was again, that tremor of memory. What was it she needed to remember? An image of a black cloak flying away swam across her eyes. No, not a cloak, a coat. Or maybe not even a coat? Maybe something less, a gown? Like the ones the barristers wore? Was she getting muddled up? Was it the drugs they were giving her? Somehow Rita thought not.

Chapter

19

"Trains, like time and tide, stop for no one."

Jules Verne

Still missing

By the time that Rita had finished telling Priya about the effects of the civil war on the cities of her birth and her University, they had crossed the town centre and were nearing Caffe Nero. They had carried on talking as Rita strode to the staff room door and popped in the code. The young women entered together and Priya sat on a chair while Rita put her satchel bag in a locker and started to don her work T shirt.

"It is hard to believe there was an actual civil war here." Priya had said seriously, "When you hear about civil wars today, like in Syria." she added, "It must be so scary for the population. A war you can't get away from. That's the worst thing. People who were friends becoming enemies" Priya and Rita had previously discussed footage the former had seen from Medicins Sans Frontiers and heard the pitiful pleas of doctors as they ran out of supplies and railed against the inhumanity which led to civilians, and even hospitals, being targeted. Rita remembered that Priya had asked herself out loud whether she would have the courage to be such a medic when she qualified.

Breaking out of her memories again, Rita wondered what was happening in the world out there. Her mother would be trying to run the dental practice which she and her late father had created, probably using work as a distraction from her worry about her daughter, Rita thought. Nayan should be concentrating on his studies and thinking about his university place, while Mohal was no doubt working on articles for the paper and maybe using his resources to see what he could find out about her. In the wider world, it was not lost on Rita that ,while she was stuck in one place, millions of people were on the move as refugees and migrants streamed to Europe from various parts of the Middle East and Africa, driven by civil war at least as bad as anything in the seventeenth century and, with the use of chemical weapons, far more deadly. Poverty, famine, violence and oppression compelled them to set sail desperately in unsafe boats, many drowning on the way at the hands of greedy pirates and traffickers. Greece and Italy had borne the brunt of the invasion to begin with, then Turkey and Hungary were affected, and now Germany had agreed to take a million, but still they came in uncertain boats, capsizing and being washed up on the shore. The EU was trying to put a deal in place which would keep refugees from Syria in Turkey, but it was unclear whether that would work. For how much longer could the world watch these tragedies unfold?

At least 40,000 people had been displaced in Aleppo alone as fighting continued, despite the ceasefire. What would become of them? How could those countries ever recover when one lot of Syrians had massacred another? It seemed that targets included hospitals and mosques, so the troops must have known the victims of their violence would include the weak and vulnerable. What was worth that?

Which thoughts took her took her back to the conversation with Priya about the civil war in England. Had all that misery and violence achieved very much? she had asked. Rita had expressed the view that it had contributed to the progression towards the sovereignty of Parliament, something the Leave side in the referendum debate were keen to emphasise. By 1662 the King was back. It took another revolution of a different kind, involving his brother, before the balance of power between the monarch and Parliament really shifted.

"It was all about power, wasn't it? Did the King have a divine right to rule or was Parliament entitled to rein him in?" Priya had dug into her memory banks.

"Broadly." Rita nodded. "There were religious differences too. Different versions of Christianity. The side led by Cromwell were Puritan in outlook and didn't look kindly on the King's side, who they thought were too close to Catholics. But even the Roundheads were divided, with some following more fundamental lines than others."

"Sounds familiar" Priya had chipped in, thinking of Syria again.

"There were factions and divisions. Sections of the army were influenced by a group known as the Levellers, who wanted a more radical and democratic state than others." Rita had told her friend.

"The Momentum of their day perhaps?" Priya had put in, referring to a faction within the British Labour party.

"Something like that, but with religious overtones." Rita had agreed. "They organised a mutiny, but it quickly ended. A group escaped to Burford church in Oxfordshire where the leaders were rounded up and executed."

"Oh yes," said Priya, remembering something, "There is a plaque to two of them in Gloucester Green Square in Oxford, near the bus station."

"That's right" Rita told her, remembering a picture of it on her iPad. "It is in memory of Private Biggs and Private Piggen. It says they were executed like their Leveller colleagues at Burford by forces loyal to Cromwell. The plaque records that they were shot near the square for their part in a mutiny of the Oxford garrison in September 1649."

"How sad." Priya said.

"Cromwell and Fairfax were trying to restore order after so many of the institutions had been swept away. The Levellers were one problem, the King another." Rita had explained.

* * *

The memories of their conversations about the King, and the Levellers, about how they tried to escape and were killed, were returning to Rita in her current predicament. How could she get away? Inaction was frustrating. She desperately wanted to get out of here. She had already eliminated several ideas. She could try to make a run for it when one of the men came in with food and untied her. The likelihood of getting away was pretty well nil. Not only were they strong looking, but they locked the door after they entered and she didn't know where they kept the key. She would have to knock a man out - unpleasant thought- and for a sufficient period for her to search his pockets - another unpleasant thought. She had scoured her cell for anything she could use as a weapon, but without success. All she had found was a row of wooden benches along one side of the room. She had become excited when she realised the seats lifted up on hinges and that the benches were for storage. But, the more she explored the interior of the storage, the more she found nothing. It was empty. She had thought that she could hit her guard with the chair if she wasn't sitting on it; then she remembered it was bolted to the floor. Could she hit him anyway? Was she strong enough? She doubted it. Her wrists and ankles were numb with the bands used to tie her, and her system was weakened by drugs. She didn't think she had the agility to bounce into life so effectively. And there could be no room for mistakes. If she was going to do something, it had to work. Otherwise the regime would be even more difficult for her- or the consequences might be even worse. That thought had made her shiver. To do it and to fail would be such a bad idea. She needed another plan.

* * *

Charles 1, the lawful king, being held prisoner, and being executed- thinking about it made Rita shudder.He could not have imagined it would turn out like that,surely? What was going to happen to her? How much longer would they keep her here? Would she ever be free again? What were her family thinking? Had her captors taken on board her plea to them to give them a message? When she had asked them, her guards, as usual, refused to speak except to use the usual phrases of command. Rita tried not to think too much about her family, about Jacob, about her uni friends, about all the people who would be missing her and worrying, because every time she followed those thoughts her eyes gathered water, in the form of tears either of frustration or misery. No, that really was not good. She must stay strong and survive this. It was what her family and friends would expect. She must not let them down by going under now and drowning in her own unhappiness. Despite her best efforts, before she could formulate any more plans, sleep started to overtake her once more.

* * *

A blue ocean rose and fell in her head again. "Justa keep on dreaming." Rita fought to wake up. It was the sound of the door opening which had disturbed her.

"Put your mask on" the deep male voice said. Dutifully, Rita raised the mask to her eyes. How much longer was this going to go on? She heard the person set down yet another packet of sandwiches - how many had it been now? more than a dozen - and a bottle of water. She felt him undo her wrists and ankles. She sensed it was the taller of the two men this time. Did she hear a sigh as well? Or did she imagine it? A sigh of resignation, of sadness for what they were doing to her? Or a sigh of weariness? Was he as tired of this as she was? A sign of weakness, maybe, she thought. It might be something to hold on to.

"Eat and use the bucket. I'll be back in 20 minutes." he said and left, while she gratefully flexed her arms and legs. Once he had closed the door, she put the mask back round her neck. She debated whether to pee or eat first. As previously, she decided to use the bucket since it would be less embarrassing to be disturbed eating than on the bucket. She washed her hands as best she could, using the small bowl of water and the piece of towel that lay beside the bucket. After she had been held against her will for a while, a toothbrush and toothpaste had appeared, which she gratefully used to refresh her mouth. Then she began to explore her surroundings, as had become her practice before her captor returned. Rita managed to eat the sandwich and drink from the bottle of water while pacing her cell, seeking for clues and ideas of how to get out.

Rita felt again with her fingers behind the curtains, where windows should be. As before she found, instead, what seemed to be flaps which felt like they were made of wood. Some sort of shutter perhaps, she thought. Maybe she could try to use the toothbrush handle to prise one panel open? It was the nearest thing to a tool that she had. She used one hand to feel around the wall, her other hand being occupied with the sandwich which she needed to finish. Her jailer would take everything away when he returned, whether she had consumed it or not.

She had just finished her exploration, and was expecting company any minute, when something unexpected happened. The room started to move. It began to sway slightly to the left then slightly to the right. Was this another effect of the drugs they were giving her? Was it an hallucination? If so, it was a very effective one, as she found herself correcting her footing in order to keep upright. Just like you did on a boat. Of course! How could she have been so stupid? It wasn't an attic at all! She was on the water. She was afloat, on some sort of boat.

Chapter

20

"Here is a very simple strategy of life: When the train arrives at the station, be at the station!"

Mehmet Murat ildan

Wednesday 4th May 2016 6pm
12 days missing

Nayan exhaled deeply, passing his plate to his brother to put in the dishwasher, the food on it only half eaten, a first in the Patel household. Padma noticed but uttered no comment. Nothing was normal any more. Nayan was not eating, and Mohal was cooking for them and clearing up afterwards. Even the success of the football team in winning the Premier League could not lift their mood for long, not without their sister to share in the celebrations.

To fill the silence, they were allowed to have the TV on in the kitchen while they ate, provided it was tuned to a news channel in case any stories developed about Rita. So various BBC reporters were droning on in the background as they went about their tidying up. David Cameron had been before something called the Liaison Committee, apparently, to discuss issues about the forthcoming EU referendum and how easy it would be to disentangle the country from EU legislation should the vote be in favour of leaving. The House of Lords EU Committee had said pessimistically that it could take years to loosen the Gordian knot of EU laws. Meanwhile in the US, Ted Cruz had bowed out of the race to be the Republican presidential nominee, leaving Donald Trump as the probable candidate and the world facing the possibility, however unlikely a prospect, of a Trump presidency, a man who David Cameron had reportedly described as divisive and stupid. There was no item on Rita's disappearance, not even on the local news.

The sports coverage included a lot about the success of Leicester City, which seemed to baffle and impress the reporters in equal measure and was at last earning their grudging respect. There was much speculation as to how this team, described earlier in the season as 'journeymen' and 'workhorses', and costing a tenth of the price tag of some teams in the League, had pulled it off. Few had seen it coming until the last run- in when the miracle seemed possible. Some had commented on the decline in the performance of other teams as they sought for answers. Was it the management tantrum with the doctor at Chelsea and the exit of their manager, Mourinho? Was it the Manchester City decision to announce that their manager would leave at the end of the season, since they had a bigger fish in view? Was it that the style of the Manchester United Manager didn't suit the team or the fans? While they had continued to speculate, Leicester had gone on winning, not spectacularly but in their own style, allowing the opposition lots of possession then counter-attacking with devastating speed and effect. A clean sheet in some games had been secured by the promise made by their manager,Ranieri, of pizza. Many times, they had come back from two nil down, several of their most recent scores were one nil. But they had gone on winning, as if propelled by the momentum which had dragged themselves from the relegation zone at the end of the previous season under their previous manager, Nigel Pearson. Now the pundits were camped outside the team's Kingpower ground, along with foreign news teams, to see what had been going on. At last there was praise for their work ethic and team spirit.

"Championes! Championes! Ole, Ole, Ole!" Nayan sang quietly to himself as he walked to the living room. He was just in the middle of another refrain, when a whistling sound on his mobile indicated an incoming text. At almost the same time, there was a noise like a guitar chord signaling the same on Mohal's, and a bell rang once on Padma's phone. Mohal had to put down a pile of plates to get his phone from his pocket, and Padma had to find her reading glasses, which she had put down while they ate. Nayan was the first to read his message. By the time he had run back into kitchen, the others were staring at their screens too.

"She is well" Nayan and Mohal said together, reading the words incredulously. "She is well." Padma repeated slowly and deliberately, reading the identical text on her screen.

"Is this some sort of joke?" Padma asked her sons as they all looked at each other in bewilderment, "It is a cruel one if it is." she went on.

"Who sent it?" Mohal asked the room.

"No idea" his brother replied, scrolling through his phone to check if the message had a phone number attached. "It's not a number I recognise" he said, pressing the screen to call the number back.

"Call it back!" Mohal found himself saying redundantly, for which he got a withering look from Nayan.

"Duh! What do you think I'm doing?" Nayan, then "Unobtainable" he told his brother.

"Try texting back?" Mohal found that, in the shock and surprise, he could bark orders but not act himself. His fingers felt frozen.

Who could be doing this? Padma was thinking, looking with puzzlement from son to son.

Nayan was on to it. But the text wouldn't send.

"'She is well'." Padma repeated. "Someone knows where Rita is and she is ok" Her heart-beat, which had been racing, started to settle as the news sank in. Here was some hope after days of waiting.

"Do you think it's true?" she did not know why she asked that, how would her other children know?

"Why send it, if not?" was Mohal's reaction. "Maybe Rita is behind it. Perhaps she wanted you to be reassured."

"Are you saying your sister may be involved in this? That she may have gone of her own accord?" Padma's voice rose as her incensed feelings became clear.

"Not really, mum" Mohal tried to mollify her. "I just mean, if she's been taken, and if she's talking to the… kidnappers or whatever…. perhaps she persuaded them that you would be worried and should be told she was ok."

"Maybe they know about the car and the blood. It was on the internet." Nayan suggested.

Padma shuddered. She hated to look at the internet. Stories about Rita were all over it, with speculation rife as to what may have happened to her. Padma had done the appeal to the cameras as the police had requested, quietly telling Rita that she was loved and they wanted her home and asking anyone with any information to come forward. She hadn't liked it, but she would do anything to get her only daughter back. The appeal had resulted in reports of Rita from across the world, but nothing concrete had emerged so far. DC Gardner had tried to tell them that no news was good news.

"What she means is they haven't found her body yet" Nayan had said unhelpfully, causing his mother to burst into tears.

Now they had this hope. This was a slender sign that Rita might be going to be ok. Padma thought, maybe she would go to the temple again tomorrow, with flowers and fruit. Anything to try to swing things in Rita's favour. She was almost tempted to ask Mohal to approach one of the Buddhist monks who had blessed the football team, perhaps their prayers would be as effective in Rita's case.

"Number not recognised" Nayan shook his head in exasperation.

"Sh*t" said Mohal angrily "Someone is messing with our

heads!"

"We have to tell DC Gardner" said Padma. "It may be an important clue."

✳ ✳ ✳

At Leicestershire Police HQ, the team looking for Rita, and the team reviewing the murder at Loughborough railway station the previous summer, were liaising informally. That is to stay, Detective Sergeant Melanie Driver and Detective Sergeant David Hann were holding an impromptu meeting by the coffee machine.

"What leads are you prioritising now?" Hann asked as brown liquid dripped into Driver's paper cup.

"Several" Driver said enigmatically as she bent to check whether the machine intended to add white foam to her alleged cappuccino. She was a trim, neat woman with a carefully maintained appearance which exuded confidence. Her black hair was parted in the middle of her head, with a fringe which just brushed well - sculpted full eyebrows in the latest 'scouse' style. The DS's hand, as she stretched out for her cup, displayed finger nails painted the faintest tinge of pink, like the start of a sunset, and her matching lipstick looked like it never smudged.

"Being?" DS Hann pressed, "This might be relevant to us finding Rita Patel before she comes to harm." he added by way of explanation, although he thought that shouldn't be necessary in a conversation with a fellow police officer.

"Sure she hasn't already? Come to harm I mean?" DS Driver asked not reassuringly as she put out her hand, ready to extract her cup from the clutches of the machine.

"We can't be sure, obviously, but no body has turned up and there are no reports of violent incidents which might relate to her." David Hann said to the back of her head as he pushed his shirt sleeves further up his arms to prevent any coffee splashing on them. It had happened before; the machine seemed to harbour a grudge against him.

"You're thinking amnesia or abduction?" Melanie Driver spoke as she stood up again.

"We have a car with her blood on it. That means abduction is top favourite. That's why we need to know your lines of inquiry. It seems too much of a coincidence that she was lifted - if that's the case - around the same time that some of your potential suspects did a flit. Suspects in a case where she gave evidence a few months ago." Sergeant Hann said as he took his turn to crouch before the coffee maker.

"You don't think she planned it then? That she's faking it? Doing a Lord Lucan?" Driver teased Hann as he put his cup under the nozzle of the machine and pressed for a black coffee. It was the only kind that, from experience, he trusted it to produce.

"No, we don't have that as one of our main lines of inquiry." David Hann replied, drily "But if we get to the point that we have to call in a review team, no doubt you could look into it."

"Wouldn't put it past her, from what I've heard." Sergeant Driver attempted a sip from the foam which was subsiding into her cup. "She has form for getting involved in unsolved killings. She may have staged her own death to keep us on our toes."

"Come on!" DS Hann was indignant as he bent to gather up his cup. "Ouch!" the brown liquid had not quite finished dripping from the nozzle and hit his fingers.

"OK" Driver smiled, "Well, if you are ruling out self-induced disappearance, these are the lines we are following on the train murder, in case they help. First, we went back to the timeline. If the daughter didn't do it, who else was around who could have? Tanisha Kahn says she was at home all the time. But there was no proof. The point being, that she should have been at home with the mother. But her mother left the house early, not long after her husband, Afzal Kahn had gone to catch the ill-fated train. The mother went to visit her sister in Coventry, who had telephoned to say she thought she might be going into labour. The investigation accepted this, having spoken to the sister. But, when we looked at it further, we found that the mother didn't arrive at the sister's until 2pm. Of course, we are checking where she was all that time. It's complicated because the mother needs an interpreter. She says she caught the wrong coach, went back to Leicester and started again. We have CCTV relating to the Birmingham coach, which she claimed she caught."

"Great!" David Hann was surprised, "You are doing better than we are for CCTV!"

"Hah!" Melanie Driver barked a laugh. "It was no help."

"Why?"

"Well if I said to you the coach looked like a trip to the Haj you might get the picture. Over half the passengers were women wearing burkas and niqabs. They could have been anyone. I couldn't tell you if Mrs. Kahn was among them or not. Really, it's the bus driver's fault for letting her on with the wrong ticket, but I expect he didn't want to offend anyone. Her story can't be proved one way or the other."

"I can't believe that Afzal Kahn's wife would be able to arrange for Rita to disappear!" Detective Sergeant Hann shook his head. "It's a stretch to think she could kill her husband. She doesn't come across as a criminal mastermind."

"Well, you wanted to know." Driver wiped a smudge of foam from her lips as they moved away to allow others to make their beverages.

They wandered to a 'soft seating' area and sat side by side on blue chairs.

"What about other members of the family? Could one of his brothers have done the deed?" Hann inquired.

"The brothers of the deceased, who run a chain of pharmacies between them, were all in Leeds at the time, with corroborated alibis. The son was at a graduation ceremony, and there are photos. He didn't want his parents there apparently. Some sort of rift, I think. He chose to study psychology rather than follow in the family footsteps and become a pharmacist, so that may be it. The mother also has a brother. He lives near Castle Donnington, not far from the airport. He works in his own car repair business and collects break downs from the MI, so it's difficult to establish where he was on the relevant day. But, even if he took a trip to Leicester, we haven't found anything approaching a motive for killing his brother in law."

"And outside the family? What other stones are you turning over?" David Hann blew on his coffee to try to make it cool enough to drink.

"Afzal's pharmacy business had recently let a couple of people go. For thieving. I guess the goods are too tempting and there is a ready black market in prescription drugs. Either of them might have killed him for revenge, although it seems extreme. We are checking to see where they were at the time. They are small fry though, and I can't see a connection to Rita." Melanie Driver told him.

"Email me their names? They might be worth a look." DS Hann nodded.

"Mmmn. Will do." DS Driver made herself a note on her phone.

"Also, Afzal wasn't above getting into arguments." she told her colleague.

"He belonged to quite a strict mosque, from what I have gathered. He would sometimes give out literature in the street and harangue groups of people - women for their clothes, buskers for their music, Morris men dancing and, recently, a group of actors doing a street theatre performance. We found footage of him, on YouTube. He is in a group of men, arguing with others about the application of sharia law."

"Do you have names? Any idea who he might have

crossed?" David Hann sounded keen at this; he needed some ideas to take back to the next briefing with DI Foster.

"We've ID'd the Morris dancing group, the busker and the actors. They were all local. I can let you know who they are."

"Talking of actors, you saw the statement from Jacob Johnson? About Rita thinking that what she saw on the person on the train might not have been a coat?" DS Hann queried.

"Mmmn. We're following it up." DS Driver's attention was taken up with a text she had just received. "Sorry." she said, looking up from her phone when she had replied to the text. "Actors would have access to costumes, of course." Melanie Driver observed. "We are checking him, but the motive isn't strong."

"I have to agree with you. To put poison in the soup in his flask - that's a personal act, surely only something one of the family could do?" he frowned in puzzlement.

"Why did he have the soup anyway? Wasn't this during Ramadan? And isn't it a strange thing to eat on a train?" he added.

DS Driver sighed. Clearly Hann's reputation for laziness was not unwarranted. He obviously hadn't read the trial transcripts.

"He was a diabetic with an ulcer. He had a dispensation ,or whatever it's called, from fasting. He was advised to have lots of small meals. Made of specific ingredients. It's all in the trial notes, if you want to know." She couldn't help adding this dig.

As she got to the bottom of her cappuccino, and DS Hann was getting ready to leave, DC Gardner could be seen approaching them, waving at Hann with her phone.

"There's been a text sent to the family" she told DS Hann. "You're going to want to know about this."

Chapter

21

"I had spent many days hungry; had slept on railway stations at times because I did not have money to pay for a hotel room... there were moments when I felt I had compromised my dignity as a human being and as an actor."

Anupam Kher

Thursday 5th May 2016 10 am
13 days missing

Detective Constable Gardner was at 10 Elm Drive again. Strictly speaking, DS Hann or another officer should have been with her. It was her task to liaise, not to gather evidence. It appeared that the local elections were sucking in resources, though. They were short-handed at the station, and Hann was otherwise occupied. It was down to her. Nayan had forwarded the text they had all received to the Detective Sergeant, together with the number that had come up as the sender, so inquiries were continuing into the message, so far as they could. On that basis, DS Hann had taken up the offer of DS Driver and gone with her to the review team briefing to gather more information on the wider family and enemies of Afzal Kahn.

Typical! DC Gardner thought to herself. She did all the work, and no doubt others would take the glory. She had to find a way to change that, if she was going to be put forward for promotion, especially with the number of Sergeant positions dropping with the austerity cuts. She desperately wanted to stay on the investigation side; the last thing she wanted was to be shunted off to sell recovered goods on eBay, although that was proving a lucrative sideline for the force. Hundreds of thousands of pounds were being raised and shared between the police, the Home Office and various victims of crime. Maybe being proactive in this case would help her career aspirations; if she could be instrumental in finding Rita Patel, that would be a feather in her cap.

Mohal answered the door this time. He opened it wide and DC Gardner passed through to the kitchen, the route being familiar by now. Jaina, Padma's sister, was there, together with her husband, Bandhu, and their twin daughters, Shona and Shreya. The kitchen was rather crowded. It appeared that his cousins were helping Nayan to prepare some sort of potato cakes and, as DC Gardner entered, it was refreshing to hear the sound of laughter. There had not been much of that in the house the last few days. There was a Bollywood film playing on the television screen; lively Indian dancing and music filled the room.

"Not like that, silly!" Shona was saying, tucking her long black hair behind her ears. "You're really scared of potatoes, aren't you?" Shreya said to Nayan. "I've never met anyone who.." she stopped when she realised the policewoman was there.

"Do you want us to leave?" Jaina asked from the sofa by the window, reaching for the remote and putting the screen on pause. The dancers stopped in precarious poses, some with hands pointing in the air, some balancing on one leg, poised to take another step.

"No that's fine. I'm just here for an update. There's nothing that everyone shouldn't hear, assuming you want to, that is." DC Gardner found a place at the table and indicated that they should all sit.

"Want to?" Bandhu pounced on the expression," Of course we want to! We are very concerned. It's been nearly two weeks. Why aren't you able to find Rita?"

"Bandhu, sit down" his wife advised. "The police are

doing their best. Let's hear what she has to say."

"Thanks" DC Gardner nodded. "You told us about the text." she addressed Nayan, turning to her left where he was sitting. "You all got the same message?" Padma and Mohal agreed. "Can I see your phones?" They handed them over silently, other family members exchanging apprehensive looks.

"Hmmn. As you said. The same message. The same number, now unobtainable."

"What does that mean?" Bandhu asked.

"The phone was a pay-as-you-go. We've established that. Bought a few days ago. It's not possible to say by who. Whoever it was has used it for the text, then deactivated it. It's what is known as a burner phone."

"That means they can't be traced?" Shona interjected. Jaina shot her a discouraging look. This was Padma's business. They shouldn't really be interfering. Those were her thoughts.

"Yes, that's right. It is interesting that they wanted to reassure you. We have a profiler working on that aspect. It may be false reassurance, but as there have been no demands that does not make a lot of sense. Does it mean Rita has asked them to contact you for example? And, if so, is she able to influence them? That might help her chances of being able to get away."

Mohal cast a 'told you so' look at his brother. He had advanced the theory that Rita might have been behind this when the text came in.

"Or it might be a trick. Or a cruel hoax." Padma put the other side of the argument. Her mood seemed to see-saw these days, from hopeful to doubtful and back again.

"Exactly" DC Gardner said, "We have to keep an open mind. But you must tell us if you get any other communications." She looked gravely round the table. "It helps us to know how organised her abductors are, what thought they are putting in to keeping their activities secret."

"They seem pretty good at it!" Bandhu could not help observing indignantly.

"That may mean they planned this carefully. Or they are very intelligent, perhaps with a knowledge of police methods. Or maybe they've been lucky. It's hard to tell."

Everyone round the table was nodding in understanding. With no evidence, the police had nothing to go on but speculation.

"If you don't mind, can we go over the list of people Rita knew, see if you have any new ideas about anyone she may have inconvenienced perhaps?" the Detective Constable asked.

Padma spoke first. "That's a long list – of people she knew I mean, not of people who might wish her harm. There's her uni friends, school friends, old boyfriends. Staff at the dental practice. People she and Priya met when they were working at the B & B, customers and staff at Caffe Nero where she worked last year. Those people she got to know in her investigations I would think you would have a record of - people at the Space Centre or the cricket ground, for example." Padma ran out of steam just as DC Gardner's phone rang.

"If you could make a list" the police officer asked "Excuse me. I should take this call" and she left the room.

"What do think?" Shreya was the first to speak. "Am I the only one who thinks the police expect us to solve this?"

"Dead right" Mohal answered his cousin. "Priya and I did some checking and put some pictures about, trying to jog people's memories, and Nayan has been busy spreading the word on-line. We could go to the City centre and try again. The main thing is to keep reminding people. They mustn't forget she's missing, to keep looking out. Someone must have seen something suspicious, or know someone is acting out character."

"We could record a song!" Shona spoke excitedly and clapped her hands at the thought. "Put it on YouTube. That might get attention!"

"Oh yeh!" her twin was enthusiastic. "We could do a Bollywood production on it!" she added, gesturing at the figures frozen on the tv behind them.

"Well, go ahead" said Mohal. "Anything to keep up Rita's profile."

His voice dropped as the police officer returned to the kitchen with news.

"That was DS Hann. He has been checking out relatives of Afzal Kahn." she explained.

"The man that died at Loughborough railway station?" Bandhu put in.

"That's right. We're thinking the trial may be a clue to Rita's disappearance."

"Why?" Shona queried.

"Well, Mr. Kahn's son and daughter have vanished." the Constable told them.

"They weren't kidnapped too?" Jaina's eyes were wide with horror.

"No, no. Nothing like that." Once again DC Gardner felt she was not performing her role of reassurance very well. "They seem to have left the country of their own volition as far as we can tell."

"Well, where have they gone? It's not one of those cases where people slip off to Syria is it?" Bandhu's comment earned him a kick on the shin under the table from his wife.

"Really Dad!" Shona said, "You're paranoid!" put in Shreya, "Not everyone supports ISIS you know!"

"No, no." DC Gardner put up her hands, trying to regain control of the discussion. "As a matter of fact, we don't know where Lateef and Tanisha Kahn have gone. But we have no reason to suspect any terrorism-related motive." she added.

"That's what they always say." Bandhu put in begrudgingly,

earning himself a hard stare from all the female members of his immediate family.

"None of Mr. Kahn's family look like they are involved in Rita's disappearance, though. We are left with what Jacob told us." DC Gardner told the table.

"About Rita remembering something?" Mohal checked.

"That's right". She looked round the table. Not everyone would know what they were talking about, she realised.

"It may be nothing, but Rita's boyfriend has said she thought she had remembered something about the train incident. Something connected to the evidence she gave last year." she explained.

"Yeh, Jacob mentioned something about it when we – Priya and I – went to see him." Mohal put in.

DC Gardner nodded. "We spoke to Jacob again." As discussed with DI Foster, the Constable stuck to the information about what Rita had recalled and glossed over the questioning they had conducted about the whereabouts of Jacob's car; that would only distress the family and, in the light of the discovery of the stolen car with Rita's blood on it, their interest in his car had waned.

"Jacob has remembered a bit more. He claims he wasn't paying Rita much attention, but now he thinks what she was trying to say was that the garment that she saw was not a coat, it was flowing and pleated, and more like a gown."

"Oh?" Padma looked confused.

"Like barristers wear in court she said. She wasn't sure she was remembering or if she'd been influenced by the barristers in the court case. But it could be an important clue as she mentioned this not long before she disappeared."

"And Jacob? Why couldn't he have said this before? Would he have mentioned it at all if Priya and I hadn't gone to see him? You know he left the supermarket early that day, the day that Rita went missing?" Mohal asked indignantly. His suspicions of Jacob aroused again.

"Yes, we are aware, Mr. Patel." DC Gardner spoke firmly, "But there is no evidence that Jacob is involved. He does his shifts at the Coop and he works other jobs. He behaves as normally as you could expect given that his girlfriend is missing."

"Even so." Mohal was churlish, reluctant to give up his theory, but secretly pleased to hear the police had been keeping Jacob under surveillance. He wanted watching, that one, he was sure.

"Do you think it's relevant?" Padma was saying.

"What? That Jacob is not behaving oddly?" DC Gardner was not following this, Mohal having diverted the course of the conversation.

"No. I don't know him well enough to make a judgement one way or another, but I can't believe that my daughter would choose to go out with anyone who wished her harm. She would be more careful than that. No, what I wondered was what you said about the coat, perhaps not being a coat." Padma explained.

"We don't know if it's significant or not. We just have to keep gathering information until we see how the bits fit together." DC Gardner was not sure what Padma wanted to hear, or what exactly to tell her. Another team were looking into the murder and the coat/no coat theory was a strand for them to pursue primarily.

"It's just that.." Padma began.

"Mmmn?" DC Gardner sensed that something significant might be about to be said, in that very kitchen, in her presence.

"Well, that Rita mentioned the same to me. A couple of days before she disappeared. She was helping at the dental practice, standing in at reception to answer calls, especially from Dr Sharma's patients. All his appointments had to be rescheduled, in view of what happened to his wife."

"Tell me about it." DC Gardner tried to encourage.

"Well, you know that Dr Sharma's wife was killed, not long before Rita went missing. She disturbed burglars. They smashed a mirror over the poor woman's head and.."

Padma shivered, recalling the events on that awful day which had been only a few short weeks ago but which seemed further in the past as Rita's disappearance had eclipsed all other matters in Padma's life. The police had called at the surgery and broken the news. 'Broken' was the operative word. Dr Sharma had been broken from that moment. They had to sit him on a chair with his carefully oiled head of dark hair held between his legs in case he fainted. He could barely get into the police car for a lift to the nursery where his children were happily playing, oblivious of the tragedy. Sunetra, one of the dental receptionists, went with him. He had no other family in the country. He had been trying for months to get permission for his mother to come over, as she could be a great help with the childcare, but the Government's crackdown on immigration ahead of the in/out EU referendum had impeded progress.

Padma and Sunetra had agreed that the latter could be freed up to provide whatever assistance Dr Sharma needed. She could also report back to the Practice on developments. Sunetra had gone to help Dr Sharma and ended up tending to his children as he was too heart-broken to be of much use, as she had told Padma on the phone. That left Padma one dentist and one receptionist short, which was why Rita, although she had an important essay to finish, had been drafted into the surgery to help.

All this Padma explained breathlessly while DC Gardner tried to look interested but felt increasingly puzzled. Sorry as she felt for Dr Sharma- it was a terrible thing to have happened- the death of his wife during a burglary was being investigated by yet another team at the station. She had liaised with them and it seemed to have nothing to do with Rita's disappearance. The team had a shrewd idea as to the identity of the thieves and were on their trail, tracking their phones from Leicester along the M69 and M6 to Birmingham. It did not seem the thieves, preoccupied with disposing of stolen jewellery and no doubt aware that a murder had been committed in the course of their robbery, could have spared the time to snatch Rita from the streets, let alone lay any plans to do so. They had certainly not been anywhere near East Midlands airport, from where the car used to take her had itself been stolen.

"So..?" she tried to prompt Padma who was still visualising that terrible day.

"So, when Rita came to the Practice to help on reception, it was a Tuesday, the only day we have a hygienist at the Practice. Rita saw Marta. She's our hygienist. She wears black overalls and the dental nurses wear white ones."

Padma could see DC Gardner's eyes start to glaze over. She had opened her pad and her pen hovered over it, but she was clearly not hearing anything worth recording as the pen did not move.

"I came out from seeing a patient. It was the last one before lunch and the only people left in the Practice were staff, plus Mrs. Parkinson and her disabled son who were waiting for her husband to pick them up. They are in so often I almost count them as staff!" Mohal and Nayan nodded at this; they had heard their mother talk about the Parkinsons on several occasions.

Interesting as this insight into the dental practice was, DC Gardner was beginning to wonder if her instincts had been wrong. Was there any point to this? she was starting to think and was tempted to look at her phone to check the time.

"Sunetra Choudhury had called in to report on how Dr Sharma was doing. We were just talking about tragedies and how they happen suddenly and Rita said to us, Sunetra and me, we were the only ones in earshot, I don't think Mrs. Parkinson heard, she was too far away and seeing to her son,

Karl...."

"Yes?" DC Gardner tried to encourage something from Padma that she could write on her pad before she got cramp in her hand from holding the pen.

"Well, she said what you just said." Padma answered obscurely.

"Which was?" DC Gardner sought some clarification.

"Well, that she had been thinking about what she saw on the train. The person she thought she glimpsed in the carriage. She was starting to get an idea that perhaps they weren't wearing a coat as such. That the dark material might have been something else. Something more like a gown, the gowns the barristers wore in court."

DC Gardner was writing something down at last, although it made very little sense.

"Did she say who she thought it was?" she ventured.

"No." Padma was emphatic. "It was just an idea she was turning over in her head. She had seen Marta in her overall and that had prompted her thinking. But she wasn't sure, and she was going to think it through and maybe talk to someone about it. Then she changed the subject and started to tell Sunetra about her plans to surprise Jacob the next day. How she was going to wear her blue sari and call in at the café to show them, since they were always asking her what she looked like in traditional dress."

Now DC Gardner could hardly get the words down fast enough.

"That's very helpful, Mrs. Patel," she said, rising from her seat. "I'll check with my colleagues. One of us may need to interview you again."

"Oh" Padma was surprised that this casual conversation could have any bearing on events. "I had forgotten all about it, what with keeping the Practice going after what happened to Dr Sharma's wife, and then Rita.... I keep expecting something else bad to happen" she was saying as she escorted the Constable to the door.

Back on the threshold, DC Gardner raised her phone to her ear. She needed to speak to DS Hann urgently. After all, he was the one who was supposed to have checked out the dental practice.

Chapter

22

"I've missed a lot of trains in my life, and another one always comes."

Lap Elkann

Thursday 5th May 2016 12pm
13 days missing

"What have we got?"

At Leicestershire Police HQ in Enderby, close to the Fosse Park shopping centre, the team reviewing the train murder were gathered round a conference table. Pictures of all the main characters in the death of Afzal Kahn were arrayed on a glass screen and gazed down on them reproachfully. All this time and no conviction? they seemed to be saying.

"Rita Patel is still missing." DI Mark Easton told those present. One of the officers sighed, reflecting the concern of them all. They knew that the longer a person was missing, the less likely it was that they would be found alive. "Because of the possible link with the murder of Afzal Kahn, I have asked DI Foster to join us." he added.

Sue Foster nodded and took up the commentary. "We think she was snatched in a white Toyota stolen from East Midlands Airport. The vehicle was later found abandoned near Leicester railway station. She was taken by two, possibly three, men. One was Asian, one was black. She disappeared on Friday 22 April, the same day that Tanisha and Lateef Kahn also disappeared." The Detective Inspector pointed to the photos of the two on the wall. "She then nodded to the officer on her left to take over the summary.

"There are no reports that the Kahns were snatched.

They seem to have walked through Birmingham airport of their own accord, took a flight to Amsterdam, and from there the trail goes cold." DS Melanie Driver, her appearance immaculate as usual, brought the meeting up to speed.

"But we think the disappearances are somehow connected?" DI Mark Easton said, looking across the table at DI Sue Foster, who kept checking the time. DC Gardner should be here. Where was she?

"What connects them is that Rita Patel was a witness at the death of Afzal Kahn, the father of Tanisha and Lateef. She gave evidence at Tanisha's trial." Sue Foster confirmed.

A young female Constable wearing a hijab, whose ID disclosed she was Rafida Hussain, stood up and drew a line between the photos of the Kahn siblings and Rita Patel.

"What was the trigger event? What made the sister and brother do a sudden flit? Was it the same event that caused someone to snatch Rita Patel? Or are these events unconnected? That's what we need to decide." Mark Easton said, sitting back and folding his arms.

"Maybe we need to take a step back and rethink the murder?" DC Karen Davies, a tall woman with short brown hair and wearing large spectacles to rest her eyes from her contact lenses, spoke. "What do we know about Afzal Kahn? His business was successful, but he made enemies. He sacked two people for theft. He argued with various groups about what was appropriate and in accordance with sharia law. He often travelled to Pakistan. In fact, his bank details show he bought four tickets for a flight leaving a couple of weeks after his death, tickets in the names of himself and his wife, son and daughter."

"Talking of tickets," DI Mark Easton said, "Did his bank account also show the purchase of his train ticket, for the day he died?"

"Strangely, no." DC Karen Davies conceded. "It seems to have been bought with cash. There is no CCTV to show who might have made the purchase."

"OK" Detective Inspector Easton was getting impatient. "Theories?" he invited.

"If it wasn't Tanisha who killed her father, could it have been Lateef? Is that why they left the country?" Karen Davies suggested.

"We checked out Lateef at the time," DC Brian Clarkson, the only other male officer in the room, objected. He was balding, approaching retirement and had a reputation for being cynical; he had seen it all.

"He was at his graduation at the time." he added.

"Not necessarily." DC Karen Davies, whose main role was to look after the IT side of things, spoke. "Look at the video footage of the ceremony. You won't find a clear picture of Lateef. Whether or not it's a coincidence, when he collects his certificate he turns away from the camera. Also, look at the photos of the pre-graduation breakfast which were posted on-line. Anything strike you as odd about them?" The DC looked round at the occupants of the table. Everyone shook their heads.

Karen Davies continued. "Well, it was during Ramadan of course. So, depending on how observant Lateef is, strictly there shouldn't have been a meal at that time. But what if there wasn't? What if the photo was taken at another time, even on another day? The curtains are closed, there are no clues to the date other than the fact that it was posted on the day of graduation, as if the meal was just happening. But that is easily faked." she told the meeting, getting a nod of approval from the review team leader, DI Easton. Ideas were what they needed and this was providing a fresh injection of them.

"But he was at the graduation!" DS Driver objected. "He's in the award picture, throwing his hat in the air like they all do."

"You know that's photo-shopped? They stop them

throwing their hats in case someone gets hurt." Detective Constable Karen Davies told the room.

"Health and Safety gone mad." Brian Clarkson muttered, folding his arms with a sigh.

"Whatever." DC Davies replied with a shrug.

"I want every picture and footage of that graduation ceremony studied minutely. Have we actually got Lateef collecting his degree? And I want witnesses checked. Can anyone say he was there?" DI Easton was interested now.

"Yes, boss." DC Clarkson said reluctantly, "But it was months ago. I daresay a lot of the students will have moved away by now. They may be difficult to trace."

Just as DI Easton was about to reply, DC Gardner entered the room, getting a reproving look from Detective Inspector Foster for her lateness.

"Sorry Guv. I was checking a few facts with the family. I see you've drawn a line between Lateef and Tanisha Kahn and Rita Patel" she said.

"Only because they are all missing" DC Clarkson said under his breath.

"I think you need to draw another line." she offered.

"Explain" said Mark Easton tersely.

"Sunetra Choudhury, the receptionist at the dental surgery." DC Gardner produced a photo and added it to the wall.

"She's not missing too? I thought she was helping that dentist whose wife was killed, Dr Sharma?" DS Driver put in. It was her job to be across all the threads of the inquiry and any related developments.

"She was, she is. But on the day that Rita was at the surgery and announced her plan to surprise her boyfriend by going to his place of work on his birthday, Sunetra was there." DC Gardner explained.

"And?" DI Easton was lost. What was the significance? he was thinking.

"That was also when Rita said she thought she had remembered something about the train incident." DC Gardner had everyone's attention now.

"I went from Elm Drive to Syston to talk to Sunetra while she minded Dr Sharma's children. Turns out she is a cousin of a young man called Virat Choudhury." she went on.

Sue Foster let out a groan. "How did we not know this?" She put her head in her hands. "One of Lateef's closest friends! They are in the graduation breakfast picture sitting next to each other!"

Constable Gardner nodded, went to the photos on the glass wall and drew a line from Sunetra to Virat to Lateef to Tanisha to Rita. She did not often get to do that.

"Do you think that's what happened? Lateef and Tanisha panicked when they heard there might be new evidence? That's what made them run away?" DC Karen Davies queried.

"It makes sense." DC Gardner nodded.

"Are you saying there _is_ a connection with the abduction of Rita Patel?" DI Easton wanted to know.

DC Gardner shrugged. "All I'm saying is, they knew where she would be on that Friday. It is possible they either did it, or they arranged it."

Chapter

23

*"People's back yards are much more interesting than
their front gardens, and houses that back onto railways
are public benefactors."*

John Betjaman

Still missing

Thump, thump. Rita was jolted out of her thoughts by a
banging sound above her head. Was it raining again? Or
was one of her captors returning? It wasn't usual for them
to bang on the roof like that. Having decided she was being
held on a boat, Rita had listened out for related sounds. She
never heard another boat arrive when her captors came, so
she concluded the boat must be moored up somewhere. That
made sense. There was no sensation of it moving through
water, only an occasional rocking, which she took to be from
the wash of a passing craft. Rita had only been in boats on
the lake in Abbey Park, so she was no expert. But she was
puzzled as to where this boat could be?

Rita could hear voices now, people calling to one another,
their voices breathless and excited. Woken from her trance,
she was suddenly feeling very alert. She noticed with joy that
her guard had that day forgotten to tie the scarf round her
mouth. It was hanging useless round her neck. Deciding to
take a risk, she took a huge breath and yelled as loudly as
could,

"HELP!" "HELP PLEASE!" "I'M TRAPPED DOWN
HERE!" and she beat as hard as she could on the floor with
her tied feet. The banging above her began again, "HELP!"
she repeated "HELP ME PLEASE" "I'M TRAPPED"

"Oi, Dave!" a female voice. She had not heard another woman's voice for such a long time. It made Rita hopeful. Surely this person was not part of the kidnap gang?

"Dave! Someone's shouting!" There was another lot of banging sounds above her.

"HELP!" she continued, thumping her feet up and down again, "HELP ME I AM DOWN HERE!"

"I thought it was empty. These boats look like they've been locked up for months." a low male voice said in an aggrieved tone.

"HELP! I'M TRAPPED! GET ME OUT OF HERE!"

"Where's it coming from?" the male voice spoke.

"It's this boat." the female voice indicated.

"Someone's inside?" the man's voice again.

"HELP. I'M TRAPPED HERE!" Rita thought they needed a prod at this point and that it was best to keep the message simple.

There was more thudding.

"There's the door!" Rita heard the woman saying.

"Are you in there?" the man inquired apprehensively.

"YES.YES.OH PLEASE HELP ME. I'M LOCKED IN. I'VE BEEN KIDNAPPED!"

Rita decided some more explanation might help at this point.

"PLEASE! THEY'LL BE BACK SOON! YOU HAVE TO HELP ME! I'M RITA.THEY TOOK ME!"

"That's the missing girl. The one on the news." the woman again.

"You watch too much Crimewatch, Diane." the man sounded sceptical.

"PLEASE!" Rita pleaded urgently.

Just as she was running out of breath and starting to lose hope, she heard another thud, followed by the sound of wood cracking, and suddenly her little room was filled with two heavily breathing figures. They were dressed like Tom Cruise as Ethan Hunt in Mission Impossible, when he descended into the CIA building to get the computer file – tight black lycra and gloves. They stood side by side, panting, staring at Rita, who stared back at them, wild-eyed and breathing heavily too. An onlooker would have imagined they had all just completed a long bike ride or a marathon run. The male figure continued to stand, with his hands on his hips, surveying the scene, the female shot over to Rita and knelt to undo her feet.

"Don't just stand there, Dave. Let's get her out. We can ask questions later." she said over her shoulder to her companion.

"You have a phone?" Rita asked as they laboured at the knots. Then the one who seemed to be called Dave remembered he had a small knife on his key ring and releasing her became easier.

"Yes" Diane confirmed, looking around her nervously as if she expected to be interrupted any time. "Let's go to the pub and call on the way."

To Rita, the idea of going to a pub, of going anywhere, was an alien concept, so small had her world shrunk during her incarceration. She stood up unsteadily, nodding at the plan and stealing herself to step out of her cell, hoping that whoever these rescuers were they would indeed help her, and that she was not just exchanging one bad experience for another. That couldn't happen, could it?

* * *

Ten minutes later, Rita was sitting on a black plastic leather-effect bench, from which vantage point she could see both the doors which gave access to the Spotted Cow. As they had hobbled together along the tow path, Rita limping and being supported by the other two, she had managed to look back at her prison, a scruffy looking brown barge moored between two other anonymous craft. It looked innocuous, not like the scene of a serious crime she thought. How strange to think she had been so near civilisation and normal life, and yet so far away.

Rita was having difficulty getting the circulation to her legs after all that time on the boat so she needed a lot of support. She was also shaking with fear in case her captors appeared. She could not believe she was going to get away. Flanked by her rescuers, they had introduced themselves to her as Diane and Dave. They did free running, they told her, or parkour as it was sometimes known. When Rita looked puzzled,they explained. The idea of running across the urban landscape, using structures like walls and bridges for exercise, had developed from military training regimes, they told her. There were parkour clubs up and down the country, aiming to make the sport fun and safe for everyone. Rita had nodded, looking up breathlessly to see the Spotted Cow pub which stood, like a welcoming oasis, on a patch of ground near the tow path.

The two rescuers had half carried Rita, so that by the time they arrived at the pub and staggered through the door they looked like they had been in a charity fundraising race. The locals inside looked up from their drinks, then looked down again, displaying English polite indifference, as if to take an interest might offend. Only the woman behind the bar expressed some concern.

"Are you all right?" she asked, her long earrings jangling against her head as she spoke, "Have you hurt yourself?"

Initially, Rita had sunk onto a stool at the bar, propped up by Dave, who ordered her a lemonade as well as a glass of water, realizing that dehydration was a major issue for her. On their erratic journey, Diane had managed to call the emergency services. Rita had heard her request an ambulance as well as the police. She realised she must look even worse than she thought. Sitting on the bar stool, she had felt very vulnerable, despite the presence of Diane and Dave. She worried that her captors would burst in at any minute. The police seemed to be taking an age.

"We should get out of sight." Diane had said, appreciating Rita's alarm. That was when the bar lady had indicated this quiet corner, not visible from the outside but with a good view of anyone coming in.

"It's not a road you see." Dave was explaining. "There are no cars here as a rule. The pub gets its supplies from the canal or by bike,- they bring things in on a trailer attached to the back."

Rita started to look frightened again, wondering how the emergency services would reach them.

"But the police and paramedics will be able to make their way here." Diane said reassuringly. "I'd like to see the anglers' faces when they come! They'll get a fright!" Dave smiled.

* * *

Once a doctor, who arrived on the back of a paramedic's motor bike, had checked her over and declared her fit to be questioned – thanks very much thought Rita, who was feeling very tired and disorientated- Rita's first interview with the police had taken place in a back room of the pub. She was not able to help the Constable, who was tall with curly hair framing her round face, very much. Rita gathered the officer had been cycling near to the scene; her colleague was securing the boat while they waited for more senior officers to arrive. Diane and Dave had been asked to wait in the pub along with the rest of the customers. "A lock-in!" one of the drinkers was heard to say excitedly.

The police officer, who took her briefly through the history of the ordeal and relayed her answers to 'Control", was clearly sceptical, leaning forward over the pub table, her clasped hands almost next to Rita's.

"They really didn't say anything? To explain themselves?

They didn't threaten you? Give you any context at all?" she had sighed a coffee breath sigh. Rita, who hadn't smelt coffee for the length of her captivity, found herself coughing and reached forward to take a sip of water from the cup in front of her. This took some nerve; as a result of her incarceration, she found she had developed a distrust of water in case it was drugged.

"Three men took you but you only saw two at the boat?" the female police officer had asked.

"I think so, yes." Rita spoke carefully and quietly, still getting used to the idea of being able to use her voice.

"Control. Three men did the abduction. Only two continued to hold her." The officer relayed. It was strange to hear her words being summarised in this way Rita thought.

"What's happening?" she had asked, feeling exhausted after the effort of escaping and only starting to realise she had the power to ask questions again, and to get answers.

"Teams are arriving to check out the boat. We don't think anyone will come back, when they realise you have been found. But there may be clues we can use to take the investigation forward." the officer explained. "We will get you back to your family soon." she had added, seeing the distress in Rita's face, "once we get the basic picture."

* * *

Five hours later, Rita was indeed at home, sitting in the comforting grey and white kitchen in Elm Drive, feeling like a queen after a soak in a bubble bath and having eaten a small plate of one of Padma's delicious vegetable curries.

"You look thin." her mother had said, fussing round her, hardly able to believe she was back, "You need to eat to get your strength back."

Hot water! Hot food! It was a miracle, Rita thought, as she sat on the sofa, warmly wrapped in Padma's bathrobe.

She had put a bottle of perfume in the pocket. Every so often she sprayed herself with it, just because she could. From time to time she would move from chair to chair in the room, rejoicing in her mobility. This new freedom was intoxicating. Her family were in the living room, anxious to stay near her, to make sure she did not disappear from sight again. A police officer had been posted outside the house.

"Just a temporary precaution" DI Sue Foster said when she came to Elm Drive to flesh out Rita's statement and see if she could give them any new leads.

"We don't think they will try to take Rita again" she told the family before they left the kitchen so she could interrogate Rita on her own. Rita wondered to herself if the officer was there in case she might try to escape. She was not sure they trusted her entirely. Or had her incarceration made her paranoid?

"Did any of the men speak?" the DI asked her. She seemed to have a checklist she was working through. This is like twenty questions, Rita thought.

"Yes" she answered, "All of them in the car I think, before they knocked me out, with some sort of substance. They had deep voices."

"Local accents?" was the next item on the list.

Rita thought about this for a moment, "Hard to say." Was her considered response, "Northern or Midland certainly." she explained, "Not southern, not London." she added.

"But you have no idea of ethnicity? Whether they were white or black?" the police officer probed further.

"None at all." Did she sound too sure? Rita was thinking. She wanted to be factual. "They wore gloves and hoods." she put in. "And the guards covered their faces." Should she mention the impression she had gained that the men were Asian? No, better not. It was only a feeling, she had no evidence.

"Tell me again what they said on the pavement, when

they abducted you." the Detective Inspector pressed, looking for clues.

Rita swallowed hard as she tried to help, "They said 'come with us' or something like that, may be, 'You have to come with us.'"

"Then they knocked you out?" Sue Foster was going over the statement which Rita had given when she was first rescued. "Yes, I was being pushed into a car, I put my hand out to resist, they pushed me and I cut my arm. Then they made me sit in the car and when I tried to shout out they put something over my mouth and nose. It smelt weird. When I woke up I was tied up, on a chair." Rita shook her head at the memory. Had that really happened to her? Although she had been trapped on the boat until only a few hours ago, it seemed like it had been someone else sitting there.

"Mmmn" DI Foster tucked her hair behind her ears as she stroked her finger down the pages of Rita's statement, as if scrolling down a screen. She is checking to see if my stories tally, Rita thought. Although she was the victim, she had a worrying feeling that the police might see her as a perpetrator. She supposed it would be easier for the police if she were in on it – it would save them hours of detective work.

"They brought you food and water how often?" the police officer wanted to know next.

"Hard to say." Rita replied honestly. "They were drugging the water, I was fairly sure of that, and I had no way of telling the time. There was hardly any light in the room" Rita still thought of her prison as a room, even though she now knew it had been a cabin in a barge. "Maybe they came twice a day?" she hazarded, "That's just a guess." she added. "I thought perhaps there were two of them, taking turns to come and see me; one seemed to be taller than the other. But it was only an impression. I was pretty woozy with the drugs."

"And?" her interrogator asked cryptically "And?" Rita repeated back.

"What did they say when they came? What were the actual words?" the officer asked.

Rita shut her eyes to remember, although she would prefer to blot out the whole episode. "Put on your blindfold. Eat your food. Use the bucket. Sit on the chair." She repeated the familiar words with which she had been greeted in those few moments of human contact.

"And that's it?"

"Yes. It was like a script they had learnt."

"And you didn't try to engage him in conversation?"

"Of course I tried!" Rita was roused from her tiredness by indignation.

"What about when they treated the cut to your arm?" the police officer went on relentlessly.

"I think he said something like, let's look at your wound." Rita shook her head. There was precious little to go on, she knew.

"They didn't threaten you at all?" Rita sighed. Hadn't she answered this already?

"No." she snapped, then regretted answering so quickly, did it look suspicious?

Within the limits of keeping her incarcerated and putting her through the hell of not knowing where she was, they had been kind and courteous, she felt. Now that it was over and she was no longer afraid she wasn't inclined to tell the police more than she felt she had to. After all, if Diane and Dave had not come along when they did she would still be there, for all she knew. The police had not had any idea where she was.

* * *

At last DI Foster logged off from her Blackberry and said her farewells. Rita could feel the adrenalin of the rescue draining from her like the water which had drained away from her bath tub. She was beginning to feel very weary.

"I am so glad to see you are so well. Rest assured we will keep looking for whoever did this. If you think of anything else don't hesitate to get in touch. DC Gardner has been liaising with your family and will keep in touch. We may ask you to come in and look at some photos, but we will leave you in peace for now. You need time to recover." she said all this as she walked to the door, straightening her pony tail as she moved.

Just as Padma met them in the hall, the doorbell rang. Padma said, "Who can that be?" and opened the door to reveal the slim figure of Priya standing there, her arms opening wide with excitement as she caught sight of Rita. Priya half ran, half fell, into the house and into arms of her friend, both shrieking and jumping up and down together, as if engaged in some crazy dance. Tears of joy were coursing down the faces of the two young women.

"I'll leave you to it." DI Foster said as she let herself out.

Chapter

24

"Railway termini are our gates to the glorious and unknown. Through them we pass out into adventure and sunshine. To them alas! we return."

E M Forster

Saturday 7th May 2016 3pm
1 day free

The Snapchat message came on the afternoon of her first day of freedom. The picture appeared and disappeared so quickly that Rita thought she might have imagined it. It was like the genie in Aladdin whose blue body she had last seen in a parade on Main Street in Disneyland Paris. Now you saw, now you didn't. It went too quickly for her to show anyone or take a screenshot as evidence.

She told Mohal and Nayan about it. "Just what we thought." they said and went back to watching the television. The novelty of their sister's return had quickly faded. It was the final match of the season at the Kingpower stadium and the presentation of the Premier League trophy. Not being season ticket holders, it had proved impossible to get in to see the match. "But we'll go to watch the open-top bus parade" the young men pledged. Andrea Bocelli had serenaded a packed stadium at the start of the game, an indication of just how far the club had come and what joys there might be in Europe next season. No one had dared to have any such ambition last summer, when staying in the Premier League was the only objective, and that had looked difficult enough.

The Snapchat photo had been of three people. A man and woman in the front, a taller man at the back. They were

Asian. They looked like they were in an exotic location. There were palm trees behind them. The weather looked sunny. The couple in the front were holding a placard, a white piece of paper or card, Rita couldn't tell which. On the sheet was written in large capitals

"WE ARE SORRY".

It wasn't a very edifying message. It didn't tell Rita much. But it told her all she needed to know. The woman she recognised from the court case. It was Tanisha Kahn; she had been unveiled when she was in the box giving her evidence. She had large eyes and a full mouth with high cheek bones, giving her a look of Angelina Jolie. In the picture, Tanisha was in western, not traditional, dress and didn't even wear a hijab. The man at the back must be her brother, Lateef, Rita thought. The police had been looking for them ever since the day of her own disappearance and she had seen his picture on-line. It seemed they had got away somewhere, that they were abroad, exactly where she could not tell from the picture.

The other man Rita did not recall. Had he been in the viewing gallery at the trial? If he had, she hadn't noticed him. He had a kindly appearance, helped by the fact that his mouth was curved in a big grin and happiness radiated from there to envelope his whole face. In front of the placard, which the coupld held with one hand each, Tanisha and the stranger had their other hands clasped together. As Rita thought about the tableau it seemed to her that the three figures had formed a heart shape; or perhaps that was her imagination, fuelled by the clear message that the couple were very much in love.

"Somehow they were prevented from getting together, I'm sure of it." Rita told her brothers, who weren't really listening;they were paying attention to the goals that Leicester were scoring, Everton playing their part by not playing well.

"And her brother got them to safety. He removed the

danger posed by his father. I just have to think how he did it when he was supposed to be at his graduation ceremony. It was him I saw on the train I am sure now."

But Rita was talking to herself. Jamie Vardy had just scored again and was having another party, according to the crowd on the television screen. She left them to it and went to call Jacob to arrange their meeting that evening. What a relief to get back to normal, she thought.

Sunday 10th May 6pm
2 days free

"Are you feeling ok?" DC Gardner, who called in at Elm Drive asked her -everyone was asking Rita that these days. "It you think you are getting side effects or withdrawal symptoms you should see your doctor." she had added. The Detective Constable had spoken to Rita on the phone the previous evening, just as she and Jacob were settling down to another of Padma's curries. The Constable told Rita that various tests were being carried out, but that they had reviewed the situation and decided she was not in any imminent danger, which was why the officer had been withdrawn from the front door of 10 Elm Drive early that morning. Rita was glad. It was another sign of normality returning.

The toxicology report had come back quickly, DC Gardner was now able to report. It had been fast-tracked, in case it helped Rita's doctors and for any clues which might help the inquiry to pinpoint her abductors.

"One of the benzodiazepine group of drugs. Probably lorazepam or something similar." DC Gardner told her "Luckily they seem to have been careful with the dose."

"Mmmn" Rita had not been sure that luck was something she wanted to think about. Was it lucky to be kidnapped? To be poisoned? Perhaps it was, if your captors were polite, and knowledgeable about drugs.

"We asked the lab to do a preliminary check on your clothes." DC Gardner was saying, "But they don't think there will be anything useful."

"Mmmmn" Rita did not seem to be paying much attention, perhaps the drugs were still having an effect? DC Gardner wondered. Rita seemed distracted and not quite herself. If it was not the drugs, perhaps it was the shock of being imprisoned? Where were her awkward questions about the police search for her? Where were her theories about why this had happened?

Monday 9th May 2016 11 am
3 days free

Rita's brothers waved and cheered with what seemed like the whole of Leicester. There was a constant wall of celebratory sound made up of cheering, clapping and horns blowing, so much of it fuelled by the confounding of disbelief, by the miracle of the win in the face of odds against at the start of the season of 5000 to 1. It was no wonder it was being billed as the greatest sporting story ever. The city was like a seething blue sea. The town centre was draped in Leicester City scarves, flags and banners, as the open top buses, interspersed with police on horseback, wound their way from Jubilee Square through the proud, applauding, fans of men, women and children. It seemed most of the population had turned out – three hundred thousand according to Radio Leicester. The lions guarding the fountain in Town Hall Square had never witnessed such scenes, not even when the city so recently buried the bones of a King.

The excitement was several stories high as onlookers sought vantage points from the height of blocks of flats and offices to watch the procession progress. The smiles on the players' faces looked like they would never fade as they passed the glinting trophy, streaming with ribbons in

Leicester City colours, among themselves.

"It is like a dream!" was a common exclamation from one fan to another, "I can't believe this is happening!".

Rita, Nayan and Mohal were making their way alongside the vehicles to the celebratory party in Victoria Park, at the top of London Road. Many families had gathered there and various picnics were under way. The atmosphere in the Park resembled that of a music festival. There were even temporary toilets to accommodate the numbers swarming to congratulate their heroes. If any work was being done in the City that day, it was hard to know who could be doing it.

The weather had played its part and stayed fine and reasonably warm, as if the elements approved of this outcome. "Will the players stay? Will they move to other clubs?" this was a major topic of conversation among the crowd, most hoping that loyalty to a team that had worked so well together would trump lucrative bribes to join more fashionable sides. There were rumours that Arsenal were interested in the striker Vardy and that Chelsea might sign mid-fielder Kante.

Nayan and Mohal had had that discussion on their way to the celebrations. "I hope they all stay" Nayan had said. "Today isn't the day to worry about it." Mohal gave the benefit of his older years. "There's the European Cup next, several of our players will be involved in that. Then it will be time for transfers, before the new season."

"How are you doing, sis?" Mohal thought to ask Rita as they found a spot not too far from the main stage, where the players would be presented to the ecstatic crowd before Kasabian, loyal supporters finally rewarded, gave an impromptu concert. "You don't seem yourself. Not still full of drugs, are you?" he teased and Rita laughed.

Although many officers had worked through the weekend, a briefing meeting was called at Leicestershire police HQ on the Monday morning. DI Foster had the task of summarising the inquiry, which was running out of clues to follow up and time in which to do it. Resources were needed elsewhere. As the team were aware, all leave had been cancelled and many colleagues were on the streets as they spoke, providing security for the crowds at the football celebrations. Unless anything dramatic turned up, now that Rita had been found alive and unharmed, the Mispers inquiry was no longer high on the list of priorities and was likely to be downgraded.

"Firstly, the boat." she began, "We know who owned it and how it was hired." she nodded to DS Hann who took over. There had been much excitement two days ago when the owner of the boat on which Rita was held turned out to be the brother-in-law of Rita's best friend, Priya Shah. It seemed like a real breakthrough. Suddenly, there was the possibility of a personal angle to this. Except that Jai, a lecturer at Loughborough University, was teaching at a university in Holland at the time and had taken his wife and child with him.

On a skyped interview on Saturday night-or was it the early hours of Sunday morning? he was losing track- DS Hann told the gathering, in between mouthfuls of a bacon sandwich he was enjoying, he had learnt that Jai advertised the boat to students on the uni website – "It's a wreck anyway, I figure they can't do any harm and there's no one to disturb out there." he had told him. That was before Jai knew the use to which his property had been put. He had seemed genuinely upset, DS Hann said, when he heard. He had let out the boat to a post graduate student, Anna Pryce, for a couple of months. She said she needed it to tide her over between rented accommodation; her tenancy was ending and the new one would not start until July. Privately, Jai had thought there might be a boyfriend involved. But she paid in advance (something he insisted on) and he was intending to check on the boat when he got back after the summer.

DS Hann paused to take another bite of his sandwich – there had not been much time to eat in the last few days- and continued. He had spent the rest of the night finding out what he could about Anna Pryce, and whether she had any connection to Rita. A call to her parents' house, a large red brick building on the outskirts of Warwick he discovered, on Sunday morning, had yielded the information that Anna was out in Cambodia doing some research work. These academics got about a bit! he had thought. Her father had heard of Rita Patel from the news bulletins but did not think his daughter had mentioned her.

It was a long shot to call the student. Would she have her phone on? What time was it over there? But she had answered. Chatting on a very bad line, he gathered that Anna had hired the boat as a favour for a student friend, Tomasz Kowalski. He had told her he did not have a bank card with which to secure it, but he was able to get the cash to pay Anna in advance, so she wasn't worried. Anna thought maybe Tom, as she called him, might be planning to use the boat for parties, but he had paid her enough to cover the deposit, so what was it to her? It seemed to be a chain of people not asking the right questions, DS Hann said.

"And this student, Tomasz Kowalski, what does he have to say?" DI Foster broke in. That was another lead DS Hann had followed up during his authorised overtime at the weekend, to the annoyance of his wife who had planned a walk in Charnwood Forest, hoping the peaceful woodland might have a relaxing effect on her husband, and planning to see the alpacas who were kept there. It would have to wait for another weekend.

"He has left Loughborough and gone back to Poland. We have asked the authorities there to try to find him, but we are not hopeful. He was in the same year as Lateef Kahn, studying engineering. It is possible that he and Lateef knew each other, but we have not been able to establish that. We have been asking around Lateef Kahn's uni friends, especially those closest to him who were doing the same course, but most were overseas students. They went abroad after graduating last year and are hard to trace now."

"If they were involved, we don't have their DNA to check with any samples there may be on the boat, or those found in the car? And there's been no luck with the clothing?" DC Gardner clarified. She knew that although they had taken away all Rita's clothes – the blue sari and her black jacket as well as the drab outfit the kidnappers had given her, which seemed to be an amalgamation of items from charity shops- preliminary tests had found no DNA or foreign fibres to help the inquiry, nothing to indicate who the perpetrators might have been.

"Yes." DS Hann conceded. "We took Lateef's DNA for elimination purposes at the time of his father's murder. There is no match for him so far."

Science was not proving helpful in this case and DI Foster wanted to get back to how the abduction had been carried out, to see if it could be cracked using photographic evidence and social media.

"They take Rita from the town centre, drug her, drive to spot near the tow path, and get her onto the boat using the bike and trailer belonging to the pub, the one they use to move their supplies." DI Foster said. "We don't know the exact route they took thanks to various cameras being out of action. We need to put out an appeal for any witnesses or anyone who may have taken pictures on their phone while on that tow path"

"Yes" Rachel King, the Constable who had first spoken

to Rita when she escaped, was at the briefing and spoke up. "We are asking around the regulars at the Spotted Cow. The landlady said they use the bike for deliveries once a week, on a Wednesday, so it would not have been noticed as missing in between. She couldn't believe anyone would take it."

"OK." Sue Foster tightened her pony tail and nodded "Then the abductors – or two of them- visit Rita every day, probably twice a day although she is hazy about that. Do we have <u>any</u> sightings of suspicious characters in the area?"

The officers round the table chose that moment to look at the floor, or the ceiling, or to stare at other colleagues, as if to say that question was for them to answer. There was no positive reply to give. In the end, DS Hann spoke for them all. "Nothing helpful so far Guv, although we have put out a request. The tow path is a place people wander along. No one lingers there. So, our abductors could have picked quiet moments for their visits."

"But they waited outside, she said." DI Foster objected; she did not want to let this go, "Surely that was a risk?"

"The boats either side were empty at the time. There were no neighbours to witness anything amiss." Rachel King confirmed. "Maybe they hid somewhere while they were waiting for her to eat and do the necessary?" she suggested, "They only needed to intimidate Rita, they didn't need to pace up and down outside like prison guards. They made her imagine that."

"Or they could have had a smoke or pretended to be on their mobile, if anyone came by. No one would take any notice." DC Gardner offered.

"Mmmn" DI Foster was not convinced.

"There was one possible sighting." DC Gardner went on. DS Hann quickly chewed his remaining piece of sandwich, swallowed and nodded, taking over the briefing.

"Uniform picked up a drunk and disorderly about a week ago. Really, he was kicking off to try to swing a night in the cells, or some other roof over his head. We've had him in the station lots of times."

"And?" the Detective Inspector wanted to get this briefing over with. "It was Geordie." Nods went around the table; Geordie was a well-known vagrant and petty criminal. Various homelessness charities had tried to help him, but he always slipped back into his old ways, as if he could not break the habit.

"When they arrested him, he told uniform that he had some information about a man behaving strangely who had disturbed his sleep the previous day. Turns out that Geordie was sleeping on a bench by the tow path, a few yards up from where the boat was moored." DS Hann had everyone's attention now.

"So, what did he say?" DI Foster was impatient to know.

"That he was lying on the bench, kipping, his feet propped up on his bag of possessions, when a young fellow arrived on a motor bike. The noise woke him up."

"Did he give any better description?" DI Foster was wondering why this information had not been passed on sooner but she was not going to ask that now.

DS Hann shook his head. "Geordie is not the most reliable of witnesses, as you can imagine. His brain has been addled by drink. The fellow was wearing his motor cycle helmet and his arms and hands were covered up. Geordie only had two lasting impressions. One was that the bloke had disturbed his sleep, the other was that he gave him money to go away."

"Really?" DI Foster could hardly believe it. It must be one of the kidnappers?

"Where is Geordie now" she asked, "We could get him in and show him a few faces, see if he recognises anyone?"

There was more looking at the floor and shuffling of feet around the table.

"'Fraid that won't be possible, Guv." DS Hann told her. "Uniform let him go, with the usual details of hostels to contact, and sadly he was found face down in the canal a couple of days ago. No sign of foul play. Post mortem suggests he had a massive heart attack and probably fell."

"Oh dear." Silence descended for a moment, in honour of the dead man and the dead end.

After a pause, DS Hann explained that the officers who spoke to Geordie had no reason at the time to suspect his story, even if true, had any bearing on Rita's disappearance. It was only on a cross-checking exercise, which DC Gardner had conducted, that the possible connection was made. DI Foster sighed and asked DS Hann, when he could spare the time, to look through CCTV for a motor bike in the vicinity of the boat's location. She was not hopeful. With the proliferation of food deliveries to people's homes, motor bikes were very common these days, and the compulsory helmet made it hard to identify the rider. Still, they might get lucky and pick up a number plate she thought.

"Now, what about the drugs?" she ticked off the next point on the agenda. The team briefing continued with speculation as to how the kidnappers had access to lorazepam and their apparent proficiency in administering it. DS Hann logged an action point to check any laptops or computers, should they be lucky enough to find any that might be connected to Rita's disappearance, for on-line drug purchases. The team were aware that the pharmacy chain run by Afzal Kahn and his brothers could also be a ready source both for the drugs and for someone competent to administer them, not to mention the aconite that had poisoned the father of two on the train. Although there was no physical evidence to link Lateef Kahn to Rita Patel's abduction, the circumstantial evidence was building up. Lateef was fitting the frame in a number of respects and remained a 'person of interest' who they would dearly love to interview, if only they knew where he was.

The Kasabian concert had come to a crescendo and the crowd reluctantly started to depart, knowing they would never see another day like this. Rita walked slowly across the grass in between her brothers. Broad grins were pasted on their faces still, while Rita's bore a more enigmatic smile. While the men relived the joy of the last few hours, Rita was thinking of something that had happened yesterday, of the letter she had received, the ashes of which she had disposed of recently, in a public litter bin on their way in to Victoria Park. Just as Leicester were celebrating their victory, so the letter had reflected a victory of sorts. But it was one which would never be publicly celebrated and about which Rita would never speak, in order to protect those involved.

Everyone was fussing about her now. "Let us know where you are at all times." Padma had insisted, while Nayan had ensured that Rita's phone could be tracked if she or it were taken. "No point making it easy for people." he said seriously. Her tutor had emailed to say she could take her time to catch up with her studies. She said her time away would be taken into account as if she had been ill. "We've never had a kidnapping before." she had written.

The letter had been lying on the white table in the kitchen when she came down for a bowl of muesli late on Sunday morning. The house was quiet. Padma was in the living room watching a cookery programme. Nayan was out earning some money as a Deliveroo rider; Rita had heard him leave earlier, knowing he would be clad in his black and turquoise lycra outfit and setting off bent over his bike with a huge bag strapped to his back, making him look like a cycling tortoise. Mohal was still asleep after a late night for the paper reporting on the football celebrations in the city which had become a week- long festival. Leicester was bathed in blue and there were sashes and scarves on various statues. Rita was pleased to learn that even Thomas Cook, whose statue had been erected in 1991 to celebrate the 150th anniversary of the first Leicester to Loughborough excursion, was joining in outside Leicester railway station.

Rita had poured on the almond milk and sat to contemplate the letter. Her name and address were typed. The envelope had no post mark or stamp. It must have been delivered by hand. Rita wondered if she should open it with gloves. What if it could provide evidence? she thought. Then she dismissed the idea. Evidence of what? Nothing that she would care to share with the police, in all likelihood.

Still, she had sliced open the top with care, then Rita had carefully removed and opened the contents, and read as follows.

"Rita

Imagine what you would do if one of your brothers was in trouble? What would you do if their life depended on you taking action? Do you know what lengths you would go to?

I think you know by now what I did, but I wanted you to know why, and I don't want you to worry that this might ever happen again.

My sister was in mortal danger, Rita, and from my own father! What was I to do? Pressured by my uncles he determined that for the sake of 'family honour' she should marry a cousin from Pakistan, despite her total unwillingness. It was not just that she had fallen in love with someone else. She had never been to Pakistan and felt no attachment to the life there while her would-be husband spoke no English and lived a traditional life in a Pakistani village. At best, my beautiful sister would have been consigned to a life of keeping house and making babies, either in Pakistan or over here. But, a distinct possibility, once they were married she was at risk of being attacked or killed, as has happened to so many brides in this situation. The point about the marriage is for the groom's family to secure the dowry, you see.

Tanisha and I talked to my father, we begged, we pleaded, but he would not turn away from his intentions. And then came the day, the awful day. He asked Tanisha to talk to her would-be husband on skype. 'You can get to know one another' he said. Tanisha said it was dreadful. It was clear to her that the poor chap had learning difficulties. He did not seem to understand what was happening. But there was worse. What Tanisha had been told would be a preliminary conversation turned into a marriage ceremony. Well, ceremony puts it too highly. But words were said which bound the couple together. My sister was appalled. She shut herself in her room for over a day and sobbed all the time. It was pitiful.

Then things got worse. Tanisha resolved to leave the house. She packed a case and tried to go out while our father was at the pharmacy. But our mother realised what was going on and she was too afraid of her husband to allow Tanisha to go. So she called my father who came racing home. According to Tanisha there was an explosive row and my father threatened to use violence. She was frightened into submitting.

My father became her jailer. He provided her with food and locked her door when he went out. That is why she could not have killed him. But the family were too proud to allow that information to get into court. How dishonouring it would be to admit that a daughter of the family had to be restrained in that way.

I was travelling between the family home and my student hall in Loughborough, trying to keep up my uni studies, with my final exams approaching. I tried to intervene, but my father was adamant. My mother

Rita had paused to catch her breath and take in what the letter was saying before she continued, her cereal forgotten and congealing in the bowl. The horrors of forced marriage were not confined to one community or religious group, she knew that. She had also read that there was help available from various quarters if you knew how to access it and were able to. Charities established to help, such as Karma Nirvana established by Jasvinder, a survivor of forced marriage and honour- based abuse, represent women from a variety of backgrounds, she had learnt. Until quite recently the only punishment available in the UK for parents involved in this practice was through the civil courts. Now there was a Forced Marriage Unit set up jointly by the Foreign and Commonwealth Office and the Home Office and, since the previous year, forced marriage had become a criminal offence. Those forcing their children into it, or arranging it, could be imprisoned for up to 7 years. Not that jailing family members was a desirable outcome, but it sent a powerful message and hopefully would deter some from trying it.

It was not just women who were affected, Rita had read. While they made up 82% of victims, 18% of people forced into marriage were men. Associated with forced marriage, she was aware, was so-called 'honour killing', a barbaric practice which saw the murder of one's daughter as less of a disgrace than that she marry outside the circle designated for her by her family. Tanisha's fears had been all too real.

Rita gave a shudder as she read on-

"What it is to have friends! They are my true family. I will not give you names but you can work out some of them I am sure. They rallied round, they were outraged, they were on my side. So we faked the graduation morning breakfast. We acted it all out, but on the day before, then posted the pics on line at the appropriate time on the actual day. That took some doing. It was like arranging a film set I guess. We had to be sure there were no clues in the photos to what day it actually was.

Then I told my father I wanted him to come to Loughborough with me on the train to make it a special thing. I hoped we would get some time alone that way and so it proved. I put the poison in his flask before I passed it to him and watch him drink it. I am not proud of this. It was a terrible thing to do and I will probably go to hell for it. But I could see no choice. I thought Tanisha could not be blamed as she was at home with my mother present. But of course my aunt went into labour. My mother did not want to leave Tanisha locked in her room all day while she was away so she unlocked her bedroom door, but locked her in the house, telling her to go back to her room when her father came home.

Yes, of course, by the time you caught sight of me I was wearing my black graduation robe. I needed to hurry to get back for the end of the degree ceremony. I had my motor bike parked near the station and sped off, arriving in time for the official photograph. One of my mates actually attended, using my e-ticket, and collected my degree certificate for me, well we all look alike to the administrative staff, don't we?

Then it started to go wrong. You had seen a figure. The police leapt to the conclusion that it was Tanisha. She had no alibi. What could we do? We wanted to escape then but she would have been in terrible trouble, European arrest warrants and goodness knows what. So we decided to tough it out. If the jury had found her guilty then I would have owned up, have no fear of that.

But they didn't and all seemed well for a few months. Then the uncles started putting pressure on Tanisha over the so-called marriage and just when we were worried again Sunetra mentioned to my friend Virat that you had said your memory of events was coming back. It sounded like you were going to piece it together. We had to get away, Tanisha, her boyfriend and me. Back to my friends for help again!

They took you from the street to your hiding place and they looked after you for a while to give us time to escape. We really couldn't think what else to do. We never meant you harm.

We just needed time, Rita, time to get away, time to escape somewhere, somewhere the police will not find us. So here we are. I can't tell you where. Obvs!

Nothing I did is really excusable and I regret any harm or hurt I may have caused. I hope you are able to continue your studies and become the fine, strong person that I know you to be. You were very brave, Rita, and very clever. You worked it out in the end."

Rita Patel returns in
Body in the Canal

ISBN: 978-1-910779-72-9

ISBN: 978-1-910779-73-6

ISBN: 978-1-910779-74-3

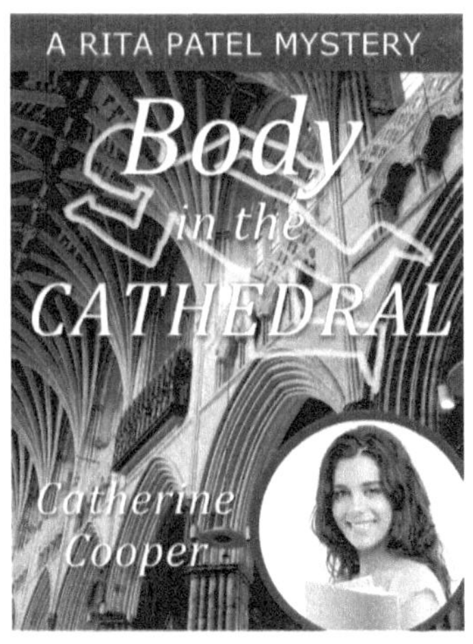

ISBN: 978-1-910779-75-0